XINA MARIE UHL

Lady Law and the Texas DeRangers

JOIN the author's email newsletter for free bonus stories, info about new releases, sales, and more at http://bit.ly/30qhIASr.

First edition

ISBN: 978-1-930805-58-3

Cover art by Beetiful Covers
Editing by Valorie Clifton

This book was professionally typeset on Reedsy.
Find out more at reedsy.com

To James Garner, Louis L'Amour, and the state of Arizona, for inspiration.
To Anne Hawley, Sue Campbell, John Bray, and Rachelle Ramirez, because without your guidance and support, my lurid imagination would never have created this book.

Chapter 1

arch 1892, West Texas

Tongue prodding her cheek in determination, Texie steadied the nail with her left hand. She raised the hammer, intent on nailing Randy Andy's wanted poster to the wall without smashing her thumb this time, when little Jimmy Fleetwood flung open the door. Startled, she missed the nail head and banged her poor abused thumb.

"God blasted tarnation!"

Jimmy was already breathless and pale. Now his eyes widened to the size of buffalo pucks. "They're causing a ruckus, Missus Cortez. Cletus, Rufus, and Shamus—all of them at once. At the barber shop right now, demanding free shaves and haircuts. God only knows what they'll do next. Help, missus! For the love of Geeswax, help!"

Jimmy had barely finished his piteous plea when—*bam-bam-bam*—a series of shots rang out down the street. A shrill, piercing shriek with the sustained volume of a train whistle followed. It came courtesy of Ellie Mae, Jimmy's older sister and the loudest mouth in three counties.

Texie shook her head in an effort to stop the ringing in her ears.

"I made it to twenty-two without being a 'missus', Jimmy.

And I don't expect to be one by the time I turn twenty-three, either. How many times do I need to tell you that?"

The sweaty lad's face crumpled into confusion. "But–but I can't call you a mister, can I?"

She raised an eyebrow at him. Predictably, a bright red flush darkened his cheeks.

She drew the blanket of calm over her shoulders in preparation for the conflict to come. Shooting rotten folks was fun and all—plus, it kept the town doc in business patching them up—but when given her druthers, Texie much preferred to use Ole Hank. The crack of solid wood on heads and the resulting cries of agony just did something warm and satisfying to her innards. She hefted the three-foot-tall hickory stick, which Papa had brought along with him when he made his way out West. The weight felt solid, strong, and overall, perfect.

They didn't call her the famous Lady Sheriff of Abalone for nothing.

Jimmy was watching her like a puppy, eager and practically panting with excitement.

"Stay here. You don't need your fool head shot off."

"Aww!"

A fierce glance shut him up quick. Texie's boots clicked on the wooden floor planks as she left the duly designated Office of Law and Order where she spent most mornings. She spent afternoons on patrol in the town or on the roads and surrounding farms, where Ole Hank got used on a semi-hourly basis.

Outside, the sun shone on a crisp, bright West Texas morning like the Good Book said, on the just and evil both. The latter few specimens were currently staggering around in front of the barber shop, whisky bottles in hand. One of them . . . Shamus, was it? The tallest of the bunch, whether that was Shamus or Cletus or that other one, looked particularly perturbed. His plaid shirt was untucked from his belt, his hair was ruffled this way and that, and half the gnarled beard on his chin was shaved off. He shook a fist at the barber, the elder Mr. Hamilton, who peered at him through the window, fear emblazoned across his bespectacled face.

"Come on outta there, you varmint! You're gonna get what's coming to you!"

"Now what, exactly, is that, Mr. Fat Mouth?" Texie put one hand on a cocked hip and used the other to heft Ole Hank to her shoulder where it couldn't possibly be missed, even by these drunken dimwits.

Shamus swung around, surprise on his grubby, half-bearded face. "Aw, dammit all to hell—"

"I suggest you watch your tongue when you're talking to me, Mister."

Shamus gestured to his weaving, slack-jawed brothers who flanked him. "Just what we need, some damn—darn—lady sheriff hassling us when we didn't do nothing wrong."

"I beg to differ. You did a lot wrong. For instance, discharging firearms within the city limits and disturbing the peace with all these shenanigans."

The flood of words seemed to penetrate his drunken head slowly. His expression of confusion transformed into one of indignation. "Hey, there! You got it all wrong. I'm the grieve . . . agerev— I'm the one that's been done wrong!"

His brothers rushed to his defense.

"It's the God's honest truth, ma'am!"

"Look at him, will you?"

"What in the name of Saint Peter are you on about?" Annoyance sharpened her tone. She didn't suffer fools lightly, and this job brought a dozen of them to her doorstep practically every day.

Shamus approached. Texie stood five feet five inches tall, a good size for a woman. But this rangy grubstaker was six feet if he was an inch, and she had no intention of letting him lord the height difference over her. Or get close enough to snake those wiry arms out and grab her.

"Hold it!"

He jerked to a stop, looking stricken. "Take a good look at me, would you? What woman will want me now, after what he did to me?"

She perused him up and down. "I don't see any blood on you. Your pecker seems fine, too, from what I can tell. What more do you want?"

He squealed like a little pig. "My pecker! No, Sheriff. It's my hair and my whiskers!"

She looked closer. Well, now that he pointed it out, maybe that auburn thatch atop his head wasn't just ruffled about. Maybe there were some jagged edges. And a bald spot. No, make that two. Add some uneven patches around the ears and that weird-looking half-beard of his. Maybe he had a valid complaint. Maybe it looked like he'd been barbered by a blind man with the shakes.

"All right, I see what you're saying. Get over there and wait for me." She pointed to the horse trough near the cobbler's shop. The scruffy brothers looked at one another before shuffling off like naughty schoolboys.

"No, the other side."

"But—"

"Go on, get."

Around the other side they went.

She ascended the handful of steps to the barber shop and motioned through the window for old Mr. Hamilton to open the door. She hated this part, the jawing and persuading and delicacy. Despite her long legs and slim form, no one had ever called her delicate, and she meant to keep it that way.

It took her a lot of talking to get the half-deaf fellow to understand. But eventually, she made it clear that he needed to get his glasses checked, cleaned, or replaced altogether. Then he ought to give some serious thought to turning the shop over to his son like they'd talked about for the last year or so. Yes, as a matter of fact, they needed to do more than talk. It needed to happen right about now. Or better yet, yesterday.

Then it was back to those three jackasses to explain the situation. They understood presently and reminisced about their grandpappy and how he went deaf and blind and lost all his teeth but was still kicking around out there in the Ohio River Valley. Heartfelt apologies were had all around and hands were shaken gentlemanly-like.

"Now as to all the shooting and hollering and whatnot. I'll do you boys a favor and let you off with one night in jail. That's fair, isn't it?"

Shamus looked to his brothers. A sorrier bunch of hangdogs she'd never seen. "I suppose so, ma'am."

"All right, then. We can call this matter closed as long as you get over there to the jail and lock yourselves in the cell. I'll be along in a little bit and see that you get supper and a cot for the night and a little relaxation to boot. Then tomorrow, you boys can be on your way."

"Yes, ma'am."

One after the other, they shuffled off with hats in hand.

She set off on her rounds, pleased with herself. Why, just a year ago, the town was a godforsaken hornet's nest, what with all the screaming and shooting and crashing about at the saloons. Most of the offenders weren't bad folks, not really. They were either cowpokes or greenhorns out here at the ragged edge of the frontier, excited about their prospects now that they'd left respectable society behind for the first time. 'Course, there were a few murderers and thieves and rapists, but she'd mainly killed them, seen them hung, or packed them off to the county seat to rot in prison.

She passed the boarding house on the left and the general store. The steeple of the brand-new Church of Eternal Salvation came into view. She stopped and admired it. Her voice, when it came, was low but from the heart.

"Papa, I'm doing you proud, ain't I?"

'Course, Papa couldn't hear her. Not since June before last at his re-election celebration. Always a sucker for a home cooking, he ate too much of that bad coleslaw and that did it. Dead by morning, and no one left to do the most important job in town, sheriff. Until she'd stepped up to the plate, a bit raw and sweet-cheeked, but willing, and that's what made the difference.

Yes, Papa would be proud. She'd kept up his legacy nicely. It hadn't been easy to clean up the wild and woolly place, but she had done it and learned a lot. Why, this time, she didn't even have to brain anyone.

Now all she had to do was keep it up, and life would be harmonious and happy for all involved, including Papa up there in heaven.

That shouldn't be so hard, should it?

Chapter 2

The stagecoach carrying Alec Malone pulled up at noon, four hours after it was due in the podunk little town of Abalone, Texas. Abalone was a hastily-erected settlement. Most of it couldn't have been more than ten years old. New and half-civilized. Indeed, the place had possibilities, but one thing was paramount above all. Alec hadn't been chased out of it.

Yet.

He straightened his string tie, smoothed down his silk vest, and ducked his head so that his fine new Stetson hat wouldn't get smudged by the grease, dust, and general untidiness of the stagecoach. With his index finger, he scrubbed his front teeth just in case the shine had worn off. He stepped out of the coach, then paused to assist Granny Smith and her granddaughter, Susie, to disembark. When they thanked him, he tipped his hat and smiled. Susie blushed to the tips of her pointed ears.

He retrieved his single piece of luggage, a fancy leather satchel stamped with Mexican designs, and looked around. The town looked like most others. The stables consisted of a rambling old barn that leaned to the right at a forty-five-degree angle. The undertaker had set up shop in a tiny adobe with a thatched roof. Over there sat a bath house with a well near the front door, Smith and Jones's General Store, and the barber shop. Plenty to investigate later. The jail was erected a few hundred yards down the street, a strange little affair built up against a tumble of boulders. Wood framed the rest of the building, which even sported a small porch. It looked sturdily built, as though it had been fashioned with no mind to the final cost. Iron bars imported from some city down the road—San Antonio, maybe—framed the windows. This town paid an inordinate amount of attention to its jail. He would do well to remember that.

Farmers, cowhands, and raggedy drifters ranged up and down the main street. A few women, too, prairie bonnets covering their heads, babies on their hips or children by the hand.

He visited the toilet around the corner from the station, an outhouse that smelled like the waiting room to hell, and went in search of his favorite place in the whole wide world—the saloon. He didn't have to look long because a few hundred yards down the street sat a pretty new two-story gem, the Desert Rose Saloon and Delicatessen. He could do with a bagel and lox, and maybe a sausage or two.

Hmm. Sausage.

He adjusted his trousers. Yes, the Desert Rose looked like just the sort of place where he would find his quarry, a fancy madame named Carlene Gibson. If it was also the sort of place where he could scratch more primal urges, well, he was up for that.

As he crossed the street toward the saloon, he spied a woman peering at him from a second-story window. Young and eager, she grinned and waved at him with all the enthusiasm of a suckling pig in search of a teat. Now that was strange. She did not appear to be a soiled dove since her hair was done up in a bun and she wore a crisp white blouse. Maybe she was just the friendly sort. He waved back.

Avoiding the biggest mud puddle in the street, he clomped up the boardwalk, the glint on his silver spurs undimmed. He could barely sit a horse, much less put the spurs to one, but they looked fine and that's what mattered in his eyes.

Alec pushed open the saloon doors. It was a Tuesday afternoon, still early. Only a handful of reprobates sat about the tables playing cards, lazy and slow. They told stories to one another or sat alone and drank with silent, brooding menace. Alec motioned to the bartender, a beefy fellow with sharp eyes.

"Mister." He greeted Alec in a low drawl.

Alec acknowledged him with a nod. "I'll have a beer."

In a moment, a tall glass of frothy brew appeared before him.

The bartender grunted. "One bit."

Alec pulled a coin out of the spending money he kept in his pocket. He took a sip. It wasn't fine beer by any figment of the imagination, but it tasted good after that long jolting stagecoach ride.

"What's the best game around, if you don't mind telling me?" Alec asked.

"Depends on what you're after, Mister. Harmless fun or bigger stakes?"

"I'm a big stakes kind of gambler, sir."

"Huh. Not surprised. Nothing going on at the moment. Next Saturday night, old Balter la Frois will run a mean high-stakes game of pinochle."

"A high-stakes game . . . wait. Did you say Pinochle? No poker?" He knew that he sounded aghast. Hell, he *felt* aghast.

"'Fraid so."

"Well, I'll be damned. I'm going to have to brush up on my skills."

The bartender crooked a smile.

"The boss will find something to keep you occupied, if you are looking for entertainment."

"I am at that."

The bartender disappeared through a door behind the bar. In his absence, Alec turned and perused the place. A fancy staircase sat against the far wall, all shiny brass railings and carpet on the steps. A beaded curtain blocked the second floor from his view. Feminine giggles drifted down the stairway.

The door by the bar creaked open. The light click of a woman's heels on the floorboards made him turn around. And Lord have mercy, here came a thing of beauty.

Bosoms that nearly spilled out of a tight yellow corset, red lips that shone like fresh cherries, blonde curly hair that looked too fine to touch. A whiff of expensive French perfume drifted about her. Those primal instincts located in his pants screamed, "Woman!"

A wide white smile unfolded on her face. "Well, now, who might you be, stranger?"

She extended a gloved hand.

"Alec Malone at your service." He took her hand and turned it over to kiss the pale skin exposed at her wrist. He made sure to gaze squarely into her luminous blue eyes as he did so.

"Pleased to make your acquaintance, Mr. Malone. I'm Carlene Gibson, the proprietress of this fine establishment."

Now this was certainly propitious. Just the woman he meant to see. He cocked an eyebrow and grinned. "Ma'am. I must say that I am impressed that such a lovely lady has a head for business as well."

She laughed. "Aren't you the charmer? I suppose I am unusual. I didn't set out to run a saloon to begin with. My husband built the place."

"Husband?" He tried to contain his alarm.

"Deceased husband."

"Oh . . . my condolences."

"Don't worry. It was some time ago and I'm quite recovered. Now let's not dwell on that. You gave me a dazzling compliment. In the interest of fairness, I should return it. Are you ready?"

He made a show of taking a breath and straightening his shoulders. "Have at it, ma'am."

She laughed. "It's just a little thing, Mr. Malone, but I admire a man with fashion sense. That makes you unusual, you understand. It's so hard to find such a creature out on the frontier, even among the women."

Oh, he understood, all right. He'd been called a dandy more times than he could remember. It didn't bother him all that much. He had a mean right cross, too. And he'd taken to wearing an iron ring on each hand just in case he had to demonstrate that without breaking his bones.

He ran a thumb over his lapel. "Straight from Tailor's Row in New York City." Unlike most of his boasts, this one had the virtue of being completely true.

She fluttered her eyelashes at him and removed her gloves. "May I?"

"Be my guest."

She ran her fingers up his chest. "Mmm. Quality cloth. Gabardine, is it?"

"Nice eye."

She re-tucked his jacket collar, then removed her glove to

slide a pale hand over the silk on his vest. Her fingers lingered on one pearl button near his navel. He felt something squeeze low in his gut. She let go of the button with a mischievous look in her eyes.

"Since you look to be new in town, I imagine that you need a place to stay."

He cleared his throat. "Yes, ma'am. That sounds quite attractive at this moment."

"We have the most comfortable rooms in town. Nice amenities such as a delicious breakfast in the morning and a full spread in the evening meal. If you're hungry in the meantime, we have plenty available to slake your appetite." She pointed at an open doorway on the other side of the saloon. Through it, he could see shelves lined with bread, smoked meats, and jars of red and green sauces.

"Most impressive, Mrs. Gibson."

"Follow me, please." She led him toward the stairway.

"You taking another poor sinner up to them ladies, Miss Carlene?" One of the customers guffawed around his remaining tooth.

She laughed again and kept walking. "Whatever the gentleman desires." She threw a look over her shoulder at him.

Alec rather liked the pleasant view of her round backside.

He did not have the capacity to do anything but follow her up the stairway. The carpet gave, soft and plush, beneath his boots, and he reached down to remove his spurs as he stumbled after her. He liked to keep fine things fine as much as he was able.

Down the hall, she opened a door and stood in the doorway as she showed a room to him, complete with a brass bed with a meticulously stitched quilt and puffy pillows, heavy velvet curtains, and a marble-topped bureau from somewhere back east. He whistled as he walked in.

"Are all of your rooms so fancy?"

She poured him a drink from the brandy decanter on a side table. "No, sir. This one's for special folks."

He took a sip of the brandy. Strong. It burned down his throat. "Is that what I am, Mrs. Gibson? Special?"

She sat on the bed, hip cocked and ruffles from the back of her dress spread out around her curved hips.

"I certainly hope so. I may be proprietress of this saloon and house of ill repute—"

"Don't forget delicatessen."

"Of course. My late husband had quite the taste for cheese and smoked meats. As I was saying, I would so like to speak with a man of refinement for a while. A woman gets tired of smelly cowpokes with poor dental hygiene." She patted the bed beside her. "Now, why don't you come on over here and tell me all about yourself, Alec Malone?"

He obliged her and sat on the soft mattress within reach of this delectable creature who, though she didn't know it, could change everything for him. He just had to proceed with caution. Not easy to do when the smell of lilacs in her hair reminded him of everything soft and good and satisfying.

"All about myself, eh? That's a lofty proposition. Err, well, I was making my way across Louisiana, in a most law-abiding manner, you see, when I heard tell that the gambling couldn't be beat out here in the sticks—I mean, the up and coming frontier—and not only that, but there were the most beautiful women the eye did ever see—"

"Ah, I see. You came for the sporting women and the gambling. And . . . ?"

"And possibly, a bit of gold prospecting out Arizona way—"

"Oh." Her perfect lips pursed. "You mean to become a stake finder, do you? Get a pick and a pan, a mule, and a bag of grub, and hoof it off into the wilderness?"

"Why not? I'm just as good as the next fellow."

"Indeed, that may be so. But I didn't figure you for the type of man who worked with his hands, that's all."

"I think you'd be surprised about all I can do with my hands."

"Why didn't you just say so? I'll call Miss Molly right on over, and she'll do you one lickety-split."

He leaned closer to her. "Why settle for second-best? I'm much more interested in a refined and intelligent woman such as yourself." If he could romance her, she would happily tell him what he needed to know, and he could have fun as well. A winning proposition all around.

"I do believe you are a forward gentleman." She leaned in herself. "I like that."

She kissed him. Soft lips, sweet breath, a clever hand on his chest and moving downward. That most greedy, devilish, and hopefully big enough pants snake of his stiffened like a railroad spike. They broke apart to catch their breath.

She glanced down at his trousers. "It looks like you will not disappoint me, kind sir."

"God bless America!" He tended toward patriotism at the strangest of times.

They fell to kissing again as he shrugged out of his jacket. Just as she was unbuttoning his vest, a horrible shriek sounded from down the hall. Loud howling followed it, and profanity the likes of which he hadn't heard since that unfortunate stint in the Little Rock, Arkansas jail.

Carlene frowned, her painted lips forming a perfect downward arc. "Those damn Harkins sisters. You'd think that twins would get along better than they do, but no, the two of them are always screeching and throwing things. Excuse me, darling. I'll be right back."

"But—"

She kissed him in a sweet and regretfully short manner. "I appreciate your enthusiasm, and I can guarantee it will be rewarded."

With that, she was up and out the door. She slammed it behind her with a tremendous *thwack* and bellowed, "Esmeralda! Fantine!"

Alec listened to her footsteps as she stomped down the hallway. In an instant, she had joined the fray. She matched the twins' foul language admirably. Shamefully? Whatever. The woman could certainly lambaste prostitutes when she wanted to.

He'd just gotten up to fetch his neglected brandy when a discreet knock sounded. Before he had a chance to answer the door, it opened and a young woman stepped inside. She pressed her back against the door and devoured him with her eyes. He absorbed the sight of her—red hair, luminous brown eyes, and a fetching figure decked out in one of those French maid outfits the women wore in the fancier establishments. She looked familiar, but he couldn't quite place her.

"Mister." Her squeaky voice held a note of awe. "I know this is improper, but I've waited a long time for a man like you, and glory be if I can't wait one more minute—"

A tremendous crash sounded from down the hall, followed by another scream.

"What now?"

"Oh, don't worry about that none," the redhead hastened to

say. "They do that at least two or three times a week. It never comes to blood nor nothing. Leastways, not often."

"That's comforting to hear. Now who, exactly, are you?"

She shook herself, smoothed down her ruffled skirt, and stepped forward to offer her hand. "Mary Ann McCullough."

He shook it. "Nice to meet you, Miss McCullough. I appreciate your visit, but I was just in the course of a most stimulating conversation with Mrs. Gibson when she was called away."

"Oh, I know. That's why I came in when I did. Perfect opportunity. They'll be at that for a good thirty minutes."

"They will?" He felt himself deflate at the thought.

"Yes, sir. I saw you get off the stagecoach just a little bit ago."

He snapped his fingers. "You were the woman who waved at me. You let your hair down."

She broke into a blinding grin. "Yes, indeed! See, I'm mighty interested in you. You're a fine figure of a man."

He felt his chest puff up like a cock on the walk. Everyone has faults, or so the preacher had often said back when Alec's parents forced him into a pew on every possible occasion. Alec knew the good reverend was right. He was as vain as the day is long.

"Err, thank you, Miss McCullough. But you really should be hurrying along now. Don't you have some cleaning to do?"

"Not really. I'm much more interested in spending time with you."

Someone screamed from down the hall. A vase or pitcher—something glass—smashed against the wall and shattered. The fighting picked up in earnest, if the sounds of crashing and thumping into walls and furniture were any measure.

"As tempting as that offer may be, I'm afraid I'll have to turn it down. You see, Mrs. Gibson—"

Mary Ann twirled her hair and gave him a coquettish stare. "I know I'm just a maid, Mr. Malone, but I do work in a whorehouse. I've picked up a few things from them girls when they're not fighting."

He regarded her in surprise. "Are you saying what I think you're saying, Miss McCullough?"

"That I want to shag you? Of course."

She approached with a pretty smile and an artless, fresh look about her. He whistled low and let his arms settle on her waist as she put hers around his neck. She made a little growl of anticipation.

He had important business with Carlene. Life-altering, even. Papa always railed on him about his lusts. Still . . . wasn't it a crime to look a gift horse in the mouth?

He pushed aside the niggle of doubt in his mind and leaned down to kiss her. She tasted like peaches and sunshine and—oh, who the hell cared what she tasted like? They shucked off their duds and fell together on the bed. Both of them giggled like schoolgirls.

That ended pretty soon to be replaced with a mish-mash of groans and sweating and creaking of the bed springs. Since it had been a good three weeks since his last poke, the whole endeavor felt glorious.

And quick.

He applied himself toward her satisfaction afterward. It must have been a good three weeks or so for her as well because she finished a few short minutes after he did with a loud cry.

Reason came back right about then. He applied his palm to her lips. She twisted away from his touch and landed with a bounce on her back beside him in bed. They looked at one another, smiling.

"That was just what a girl needed."

"Amen to that."

As they lay there catching their breath, it occurred to him that the girls down the hall had stopped their shrieking.

The door flung open. Carlene stood on the threshold. Her mouth hung open for a breath or two. Alec leapt to his feet buck naked. Mary Ann dove for her uniform.

Carlene's carefully made up face turned beet red. "How dare you—"

Mary Ann squealed.

Alec tried to explain. "We were just conversating—"

"Conversating with your penis!" Carlene fired back.

It was a talented organ, he had to admit. But not that talented.

Carlene's fingernails poised like eagle talons.

Alec didn't know what went on in hell. It probably involved a lot of uncomfortable things to do with one's fingernails, genitals, and buttocks. Carlene flew at him, and he figured he was about to find out.

* * *

Texie was striding back to the sheriff's office when a commotion over at the Desert Rose caught her attention. Lord Almighty, it sounded like someone was skinning a passel of cats. Yowls and high-pitched shrieks and crashing about. Which was to say, a louder sort of chaos than usual on a Tuesday afternoon.

She rushed through the batwing doors just in time to see

a naked man tumble down the stairway. His pale white ass flashed on each revolution. He landed Indian fashion at the bottom of the stairs, eyes crossed and blood leaking from the corner of his lips.

She took in the looks of him. A whole lot of lean muscles, the occasional mole, a nicely defined waist, the outline of which pointed down in a vee to . . . well, no need to examine that since the fellow might soon be dead if the violence of that fall was any indication.

He shook his head and his eyes righted themselves.

All right, then. He would likely live another day.

Carlene Gibson and that new maid, Mary Ann, appeared at the top of the stairs. They clawed at one another and lurched around, screeching like owls in flight. Only louder. Carlene had lost a shoe, and the sleeve of her fine ruffled dress had been ripped clean off. Mary Ann's red hair stuck straight out like a flag. Her uniform gaped open at the chest and her udders swung around with each lurch and blow. The women's flailing tore the beaded curtain, and glass beads scattered everywhere.

Carlene shoved the maid aside with an indelicate grunt and dashed down the stairs to pounce on the naked man like an enraged polecat. Long red wheals appeared on his biceps and chest and marred his all-too-pretty face before he captured both of her wrists with one hand. Then she set to kicking him. Her face looked like that of a devil from the fiery pit—red and puffy, teeth bared, with eyes that shone with downright evil glee.

The stranger managed to haul himself upright, but his considerable height advantage over her did him little good. She aimed the pointed tips of her laced-up boots at his shins. He twisted around to avoid that fierce foot of hers, but she struck his shins with uncanny accuracy.

Texie slapped Ole Hank on the brass railing so hard that it rang like the Liberty Bell. "What in the Sam Hill is going on here?" She used her deepest, most commanding voice.

No one paid a lick of attention to her. In fact, it seemed to spur the women on!

Carlene kneed the man in the love hatchet. He let out a high-pitched shout that ended in a pitiful mewl as he bent over at the waist and attempted to protect himself with his free hand. From the scrunched up look on his face and the sweat popping out on his forehead, he wasn't having much luck.

Carlene ripped her hands free from the poor unfortunate's grasp and went for his ears. She seemed intent on ripping them clean off.

"Get your hands offa my man!"

Mary Ann leapt again at Carlene. The lot of them fell to the floor in a mass of writhing bodies.

Texie didn't much like using Ole Hank to brain women, so she jabbed it in between the bodies and levered it with a hard yank. The women flew one way and the stranger flew another. Before they could scramble up again, she brought Ole Hank up to her shoulders in a horizontal position and rammed into them with all her strength.

Somebody yipped. Someone else took the name of Baby Jesus in vain. A third person whimpered like a half-smashed goat.

"Get over here and help out!" Texie commanded the dumbstruck saloon patrons.

Several lanky cowhands rushed into action, and within a breath or two, all three of the combatants had been restrained.

With undiminished enthusiasm, the women continued to

hurl invectives at one another. Two whippersnappers held up the naked gentleman, who sagged between them. He looked a sight. Haggard and streaked with scratches, a goose egg rising on his temple from that tumble down the stairs, and half of the patch of chest hair on his sternum ripped clean off. A quick glance at his nether regions told her that they'd survived mostly intact. Some future female would likely find that most pleasing. That and his smooth jaw, which had a nice manly cut to it.

A moment later, and he'd recovered enough to draw himself upright. He didn't seem intent on violence himself, so she nodded at the cowboys to let him loose. He adjusted that fine jaw of his and shook himself like a horse who'd just finished rolling around in the dirt. She saw the moment he noticed her. His eyes widened and he slicked back his light brown hair. He straightened up to his full, impressive height. A smooth grin unfolded across his face.

"Who do we have here?"

She snorted. Men!

The chaos started again when Carlene tore free of her imprisoners and grabbed Mary Ann about the throat. Lusty throttling ensued. The noise of the gathered crowd rose in pitch, and Texie flung herself at the she-cats again.

One of the women pulled her hair and stomped on her instep with a pointed high heel. A bony elbow made jarring contact with her ear, but Texie managed to separate them without further injury.

It took four men to pin Carlene down that time.

"Somebody tell me what's going on!" Texie demanded.

Female voices chorused.

"She's a whore!"

"He's a bastard!"

"She tried to stab me with an eyebrow plucker!"

"It was a nail file, you dimwit!"

Texie glanced at the newcomer. He shrugged, a 'what, little old innocent me?' look on his face. His brilliant blue eye—the one that wasn't swelling up—twinkled.

"He attacked my girls!" Carlene shrilled. "Hang him high, Sheriff!"

"I did no such thing!" His eyebrows wrinkled up and his lips flattened. "You're the sheriff?"

"You got something you want to say about that?" Texie snapped.

He gave a little shrug. "No, ma'am. A woman can surely lock up miscreants as good as a man, I suppose."

"Not about that, you jackass. About assaulting Mrs. Gibson's girls."

He drew himself up indignantly. "I have never assaulted a lady of the evening in my life. Look at me. Why would I need to get after a woman? They get after me quick enough themselves."

Texie restrained herself from rolling her eyes. Instead, she tried to look impressed and stepped up to him, adding a swish to her hips.

"You got a point there, Mr. . . . ?"

He extended his hand. "I'm Alec Ma—"

She flipped out her handcuffs—fastest draw in the West—and snapped them on one of his wrists.

"Hey! What's this all about?"

Texie jerked his handcuffed arm behind his back and locked the other wrist, too. "You're under suspicion for assault. Don't make it resisting arrest, too."

She took his firm, muscled upper arm and hauled him out the door.

Chapter 3

Texie led Alec the troublemaker down Main Street. He didn't resist. Leastways, not physically.

"Now, sheriff, you've got it all wrong. I'm the assaulted party in the first part. Here I am, an innocent traveler who wants no more than a spot to rest his weary—but exceedingly well-groomed—head. How could I know what a hotbed of debauchery and violence Abalone would turn out to be? I was in danger from the instant I stepped through the saloon door—"

"Where you were just looking for an innocent bit of card sharking," Texie speculated.

"Now, that's an offensive opinion. I take especial care to be forthright and scrupulous in all of my gambling activities."

She dragged him to a halt. "Enough. I know a skinflint when I see one. So start telling me the truth or I may break out my rusty old neck irons and give them a go."

His eyes flicked from her scuffed boots to her well-worn denims and up to her blue chambray shirt with the tin star on her breast. "You mistake me, ma'am. I would never try to deceive the law. Especially someone like yourself, the loveliest peace officer I've ever seen." He paused.

She raised her eyebrows. "You expecting me to say, 'thank

you'?"

"Most women do."

"Most women are idiots."

At that point, Texie realized that they were making a spectacle of themselves. Passersby stopped in their tracks and gaped. Chigger Antoine, who usually drove his buckboard like the devil was chasing him, yanked the reins to a stop to give them an exaggerated double-take.

Alec nodded at a few of the folks and even flashed his teeth at Widow Anderson, who gave an indignant yelp and covered her eyes. She would have walked right into the horse trough if Reverend Rogers hadn't steered her clear.

"A modest bunch, are you?" Alec observed.

"It's not every day that some duded up jack-o-lantern strides down main street naked as the day he was born."

He appeared to consider her words. "Apparently so. Never can say that I care much about being naked. In fact, I'd run around naked all the time if the sun didn't burn my bits."

She stopped a half dozen yards from the jail and considered his manhood with a sigh and a little shake of her head. "Not sure I would flaunt that around, if I were you. It's a little raggedy, ain't it?"

He hunched to look for himself. "It's the same as it ever is. Ah, shame on you, Madam Sheriff. I see what you're doing. Teasing me."

She shrugged and concealed a grin.

When they made it to the jailhouse, she shoved him in the door first. She pointed at the wooden chair in front of her desk. "Sit."

A glance at the two jail cells in the back told her that the three hell-making brothers from this morning had dutifully locked themselves up. Cletus snored on the cot while Rufus lay curled on the floor, his jacket clutched in his arms like a child holding a blanket. Shamus lounged up against the bars. He craned his neck to see.

"Howdy, sheriff. Who you got there? Some poor soul what lost his knickers?"

"Something like that."

"Need help batting him around?" Shamus cracked his knuckles.

"Maybe. I'll let you know if it comes to that."

"Yes, ma'am."

"You just relax now while I interrogate this ne'er-do-well."

Shamus gave a disappointed sigh but continued watching as if he was in the front row of a burlesque show.

She gestured at the seat in front of the desk, then took her place behind it. Alec leaned in, all earnest in a bootlicking way. "Sheriff, you must realize that this is all a misunderstanding of epic proportions."

Now that she was no longer distracted by his state of undress, she got a good look at his easy, soft mouth. It probably got that way from continual use.

"Truly, astoundingly, unconditionally epic."

"Do you ever shut up, Mister Ma?"

"The name's Malone, sheriff."

"My mistake."

He sat back and regarded her with a faint grin. She hadn't noticed it before, what with all the hollering and carrying on, but he had a low, smooth voice. "The answer to your question is 'yes', by the way. On occasion, I have been known to quiet down."

"Like when you're asleep?"

He crinkled his forehead as if pondering the question. "Not always, according to many of my companions of the evening."

She leaned her elbows on the desktop. "Yes, Mr. Malone. I imagine that the brawl I just hauled you out of had something to do with your companions of the evening—er . . ." She looked over at the clock on the wall. "Afternoon. Now, why don't you tell me the whole story?"

He launched into a ridiculous tale that made him out to be as innocent as Baby Jesus and twice as holy. It was peppered with phrases like "concerned for the lady's honor" and "conversing in the sitting room" and "inquiring about the gentle disagreement of the Harkins sisters."

Texie sat through that load of bullshit silently for a good ten minutes until it seemed that it would continue into the night. She held up a hand.

"Let me get this right, Mr. Malone. You arrived on the noon stage from points east. At four pm, I believe. It's now 5:47 pm. In a period of . . ." She calculated. "One hundred and seven minutes, you managed to set up house, poke one woman, half-poke another, and arouse such feelings of jealousy in the two of them—neither of which you had even met before today—that they threw you down the stairs bare-ass naked and set to savaging each other."

He shrugged. "It's a burden, being this fine. But it's one I've got to bear."

"A burden that is going to get you a few nights in jail."

He jolted upright. "Now, sweetheart, let's talk about this."

She rested her elbows on the desk and leaned in so he could hear her clearly. "I'm sure you're used to talking your way out of all kinds of things, Mr. Malone. You're not gonna talk your way out of this one."

Incredibly, he shut up. She examined the most wanted posters on the wall, making a big deal out of examining Malone's face, then studying each poster. That one was too skinny, that one too ugly, another had a blade-like nose that could gut folks from a yard away. One of them was Ma Kettle. Texie cocked a considering eyebrow at Malone. Nah. Not even close. She knew the others by heart, and none of them fit the bill either. Dang it. She reached into the left-hand desk drawer and slapped the stack of less-well-known wanted posters there in front of her. One by one, she thumbed through them, taking her time trying to find a match.

"Turn your chin to the right, will you?"

"It's not my best side."

"Let me guess. That's your backside."

He chuckled. "I like your wit, sweetheart. Mind if we chat a bit while you're figuring out whether I'm a bank robber or some other kind of miscreant?"

She glanced up at him. He appeared calm and confident. Probably an act. He didn't seem dead-eyed enough to do something truly evil, but he annoyed her so thoroughly that she didn't mind making him squirm in his seat.

"Have at it." He wouldn't be the first to talk himself into confessing some foul deed or another.

"Being that I'm new in town, I'm curious about the place. Tell me about the town luminaries. The founders and business owners and local residents. You've been here all your life, if I'm not mistaken."

"Yup."

"I've come a long way to this little town, and I just might be here for some time. I'd like to learn about who's who and what's what."

He looked at her expectantly but she kept her mouth shut.

"Honest curiosity, sheriff. You don't begrudge me that, surely?"

"Nope. Doesn't mean I have to indulge it, though."

"I will!" called Shamus.

Texie gave a dismissive gesture. "Be my guest."

Malone struggled out of the chair—still cuffed—and leaned against the door frame to the back room.

Apparently, Shamus liked to talk almost as much as Malone did. He went on about the banker and aspiring bowling alley owner, Harkins, and Maybelline, the widowed postmistress general with fourteen kids.

Texie spoke up. "She's over at city hall."

Malone's eyebrow raised, questioning.

"Just in case you want to romance her, too."

"Err, noted."

Shamus blathered on about Cherry Jenkins with his ranch of seven thousand head of cattle and two hundred cowhands before he got to Beauregard Gleason, the owner of the Crystal Palace Saloon and Whorehouse and the oiliest, slimiest, most horrid man in west Texas. If Texie could find a statute to lock a fellow up on pure repulsivity, she would do so in a heartbeat.

Shamus studied the bars holding him and his brothers in place. "Why, ain't Mr. Gleason the one that paid for this jail all by himself?"

Texie grunted.

If Malone had been a mule, his pointed ears would have swiveled around in interest. "Oh, so he's a wealthy individual, is he?"

It was time to nip this line of inquiry right in the bud. She dug around in her desk drawers for an extra bandana, the faded blue one. When she found it, she took off the new red one from around her own neck and tied two ends together.

"Come on." She gestured for Malone get up and come over to her, which he did like a cock of the walk, shoulders high and that damn ever-present smirk on his face.

"Closer."

"Yes, ma'am." He drew out the 'ma'am'.

Shamus chortled.

She scowled at Shamus, who shut his mouth quick as could be. The blood rushed to her face as she leaned forward in the creaking banker's chair and reached around his slim waist to knot the other ends of the bandanas together so that the rectangular cloths gave him scant decency. He smelled like dust and fancy toilet water. She didn't much like being so close to him, feeling the heat of his body and the weight of his amusement as he looked down on her. *Don't look up at his face. Don't. Do NOT.*

She looked up. His light blue eyes softened and his lips parted. She recoiled rattlesnake-quick to put a couple of feet between them.

A moment of silence reigned while he watched her. Then, "Why, thank you, Miss . . . ?"

She eyeballed him. The teasing, nothing-can-touch-me glint had returned to his eyes. "This isn't a social call."

"Is that the only way you'll give me your name?"

"Texie Cortez."

He nodded at her, then gestured with his chin at the stack of posters on her desk. "Looks like you're done investigating me."

"I could probably lock you up on lewdness alone."

"I doubt it. In fact, you're not gonna charge me with anything, are you? I know my rights, Sheriff."

She stood up and folded her arms, now at a safer distance. "You some sort of lawyer, Mr. Malone?"

"Not exactly. Though my father back in New York City is a district judge. Once upon a time, he had it in his head that I was gonna be a lawyer just like him. I even went to lawyer school for a whole long, wretched year. It didn't stick."

His voice had a certain confidence in it that struck her as truthful.

She went to the wavy window panes to look into the street beyond. "As much as it pains me to admit it, I don't have anything to charge you on. Except maybe vagrancy. That's good for at least one night in a cell."

"I can't be a vagrant if I have a room over at the saloon."

"Doesn't look like you do anymore." She nodded out the window.

He looked where she indicated. "Damn it all! Sheriff, I'm gonna need to take care of this—"

"Go ahead." She fished the handcuff keys out of her breast pocket and unlocked his wrists.

He hissed and rolled his shoulders now that his arms were free. "I would tip my hat at you if I had one, Sheriff." He flashed a genuine smile at her, then dashed out the door, the bandanas around his waist flapping in the breeze.

She heard him call to Carlene, "Now, sweetheart, let's talk about this."

From the window, she watched Carlene throw his clothes out the saloon's second-floor window. They fluttered to the muddy street. His valise followed. It landed with a crack and a thud atop the hitching post.

"Burn in hell, you sleazy bastard!" Carlene yelled.

Alec scampered around in a bid to snatch britches and boots and white shirts out of the mud. Texie watched for longer than she should have, considering his state of undress.

He was something else, this Alec Malone. A smooth talker with smarts to boot. A thorough-minded rascal if she ever saw one. No, she didn't have anything to charge him with. But if he stayed, that would change pretty quickly.

She was sure of it.

Chapter 4

lec crept through the back door of the Desert Rose Saloon and Delicatessen first thing the next morning. Only the most industrious townspeople were up, frying flapjacks or saddling workhorses for the long day's labor ahead.

Inside the saloon, a few grizzled old drunks sat around a table. They jawed and sipped coffee from the pot on the corner stove. No one else looked to be around. Good. Alec debated whether he should crawl behind the bar until he reached Carlene's office door or if he should walk to it like a respectable man.

A donkey brayed somewhere nearby, then brayed some more. The old drunks chuckled and hollered out to Farmer John, a passerby, to go find the unhappy equine and shut it up. Farmer John had no such inclination, or so the exchange of vulgar but lighthearted words indicated.

The doings outdoors so occupied the codgers that Alec snagged a steaming hot cup of brown gargle. He squared his shoulders and approached the office door. If it's one thing his illicit adventures had taught him, when you looked and moved like you were supposed to be somewhere, most people didn't bat an eye at you.

The door was locked, but he bumped it with his knee in the precise spot to pop the lock open. Inside, the neatly kept room smelled like Carlene's perfume.

An hour and a half later, after he had snooped in every last nook and cranny and risked two more cups of coffee—and one dash to see a man about a horse—he heard Carlene's heels clip-clopping across the wooden floor. He plastered himself against the wall beside the door. She walked in with her arms full of ledgers and froze like a deer scenting danger.

"Good morning, Mrs. Gibson."

She spun around, and one of the ledgers slid off the stack to land on the floor with a *thump*.

Her eyes hardened. "You!"

He moved in front of the door to block her immediate escape.

Before she could fling the remaining ledgers at his head, he took his hat off and attempted to appear contrite. "Please, hear me out. I realize that I am a low-down, dirty skunk for what I did to you. As sorry as a duck in a drought. My repentance must be but little consolation for the humiliation you endured on my behalf. That shame will follow me to my grave. I hope, though, that you can forgive me, although I will understand if you cannot. Please accept this humble token as a measure of my contrition." He reached into his jacket pocket to produce the lace handkerchief he'd bought at the Ladies' Emporium back in Baton Rouge for whatever woman-related incidents might occur in the future. He handed it to her.

She put the ledgers on the desk and smoothed a thumb over its expensive, delicate design. Then she looked him in the eyes. Hers glowed like flames as she dropped it on the floor and stamped on it with one of her delicate high-heeled boots. Her voice sounded like cut diamonds. "Give me one reason I shouldn't call my men down on you."

He thought lightning fast. "Money."

She drew in a breath that probably would have resulted in a sharp, biting retort if she hadn't thought twice. "State your case."

All right, then. Time to make it good. "I've been around for awhile, seen a few things. Been a few places. And one thing I know is that out here in the wilderness, there's not a lot of excitement that doesn't involve stampedes or dying of cholera. But when somebody like me comes along, a handsome stranger with a slick card game, well, darlin', that's a sensation. I've seen many a bored cowpoke dash into a saloon after the merest suggestion of unusual entertainment, not to mention the prospect of handing his hat to some city slicker while fleecing him of his greenbacks. I can guarantee you the Desert Rose will be the talk of the range if you let me set up some games here."

"Aren't you full of yourself?"

He shrugged. "Nothing wrong with the truth. Consider how many drinks you'll sell and how many painted ladies you'll put to work just by letting me run a few games here."

She folded her arms. At least she hadn't ordered him flayed alive. Always a promising sign.

"We may be able to strike a deal, Mr. Malone. But I require complete honesty if that's the case. You're hiding something from me. I'm certain of it."

The way she regarded him with those sharp, unforgiving eyes made his chest tighten and his smirk feel forced. He wanted to lie until he got back into her good graces, but part of being a good gambler meant knowing when to throw down the cards.

"You got me, Mrs. Carlene. I have a big problem, and you're the only one who can help me out of it."

She leaned back against the desk top. A look of superiority unfolded across her flawless features. "Go on."

"I have it on good authority that your fine establishment is the favored place of entertainment for Snarly Pete and the Bully Flamenco gang."

She didn't blink an eye. "You're mistaken about that. I've never met any of those scoundrels."

"Let me rephrase that. I have it on *unimpeachable* authority that Snarly Pete and his outlaws take over the whole joint every now and again when they feel the itch to have some female companionship."

She studied his face. "For the sake of argument, let's imagine that I do have a nodding acquaintance with Snarly Pete. Why do you care?"

"I have an urgent need to make contact with the esteemed gentleman. And you, my beautiful flower, are the key."

"I'm not turning him in for his bounty, if that's what you're thinking."

The bounty? How odd that this possibility had never even crossed his mind. "Nothing like that, I assure you. I'm looking for a man, and Snarly Pete is the one who knows how I can find him."

"Jilted lover?"

He nearly choked. "No!"

"You're not going to tell me who you want to find and why?"

He flicked a spot of fuzz off his trousers. "If that were relevant to our negotiations, I would tell you straight out. It isn't, though, and I won't."

"I see." Her gaze penetrated him for an uncomfortable

instant. "I suppose I can allow you some slight measure of privacy. And I could even be convinced to assist you in your endeavors to find Snarly Pete and his gang. For a price."

He jammed his fist in his pocket and drew out his money pouch. He tossed it to her. "Five hundred dollars, earned by the honest sweat of my brow. I believe you will agree that this is a generous fee for a tiny bit of information that will in no way ever be traced back to you."

She weighed the pouch in her hand. "Oh, it had better not in any way ever be traced back to me. I can be ruthless when I'm double-crossed."

"I don't doubt it, ma'am. You are a formidable presence."

She crooked a grin at him. "I agree. Five hundred dollars is a generous amount. For a deposit."

"Now, hold on there."

She pushed herself off the edge of the desk and strode toward him. "I will not hold on there, you skinflint. You think you can crawl in here and flash your blue eyes and I will fall into your arms? After what you did to me? Oh, no, Mr. Malone. You are going to pay, and pay dearly. I want five thousand dollars."

"But—"

"It's my final offer. No, actually. Let me rephrase that. It's my *only* offer."

He let out a breath. His voice broke when he spoke again. "You're as tough as you are beautiful, Mrs. Carlene. That five hundred about cleared me out. It will take me awhile to earn five thousand, but if I can start tonight I'll get to it."

"Certainly. Start tonight. But not here. I want payment in full before you show your smug face in here again. Then I'll tell you what you want to know about Snarly Pete."

"Hey—"

"Also, you have three days to get me the money or the deal's off."

"Three days! How am I supposed to come up with forty-five hundred in three days? You won't even let me sit at your tables."

She smiled. "I haven't the slightest idea, Mr. Malone. But I suggest you think of something as soon as possible. Now, kindly get out before I call my boys in here to throw you out."

Alec knew he'd pressed his luck as far as it would go. He flew out the door like a scalded dog.

Out on the boardwalk, the full distressing reality of his situation slammed into him. He stumbled along, head spinning. He had to get to Snarly Pete, and Carlene was his best, most accessible source. But this two horse town likely didn't have enough well-heeled rubes to generate that kind of cash.

Someone fell into step beside him. Long shapely legs and boots with abalone tips on the ends. Texie.

"You look unhappy, Mr. Malone. What's the problem?"

He glanced at her. She looked straight ahead, but a dimple showed in her left cheek. A scent like cinnamon wafted around her. He wished he didn't find it quite so enchanting.

"Nothing I can't handle," he lied. He faked a teasing tone. "Couldn't stay away from me, eh, Sheriff? It's happened to me before. You're sweet on me, aren't you?"

She stopped in her tracks. "It's true. Your head really is as fat as your mouth."

He crossed his hands over his heart. "You wound me, woman."

"I wish."

"That's what they all say."

She regarded him, her gorgeous plump lips twisted into a

most unflattering frown. "I think you should listen to me very closely, Mr. Malone. I know who you are. What you are. A low down, mangy con artist. I've seen your like a dozen times or more, and never once did any one of those cretins turn out to be worth a damn. So listen up. I don't know why you're here, but I am going to find out, and when I do, I will throw your ass out of town so quick that you won't know what hit you. You hear me?"

He swallowed. "Yes, ma'am."

"Good. Go about your business now. And I'll be seeing you soon." She stepped back and spoke loud enough for passersby to hear. "Have a pleasant afternoon, Mr. Malone."

He watched her stride off, her words echoing so loudly in his head that he couldn't even properly appreciate her rump. A truly tragic state of affairs.

He had plans to make, and they didn't involve a delectable sheriff, unfortunately. Time was already running short. He straightened his shoulders and headed toward the town's other saloon.

Chapter 5

The saloon door swung open and clattered shut, enough off kilter that it made a squeaking racket every time someone used it. Alec forced the annoyance aside to concentrate on the matter at hand, Merle, the sweaty, odiferous ranch hand across the table from him.

Merle had black eyes, a cowlick, and a left hand with only three fingers. When he saw Alec look at his hand, he crowed, "Rope got wound around my two middle fingers and the heifer got spooked. Ran away like a jackrabbit. Popped them fingers right off. The other boys and I buried 'em that night. Had a ceremony with gospel music and all."

Speaking of hands, Alec had let him win the first two, like he always did in such situations. Merle's cheeks flushed when he had a great hand, and when he had a bad hand his forehead and neck broke out in rivulets of perspiration. A couple of obvious tells when one knew what to look for. And Lord have mercy, but sweat stained Merle's hairline right now.

Alec tapped the table with his cards and squinted at his opponent. Squinting made him appear to ponder whether to risk a play when instead, he had decided to toss his pair of eights against Merle's double deuces a good six minutes ago. A few bar fights had taught him that a lot of people found it downright arrogant when he flung cards down an instant after his opponent blundered. Although perhaps his blinding, triumphant grin had something to do with that perception, too.

"I may regret it, but I'm gonna play." Alec licked his lips in a nervous manner. Hesitantly, he laid his hand down on the table.

"Gol darn it!" Merle tossed his paltry twos in front of Alec.

"What a fortuitous turn of events!" Alec gathered the $87-odd dollars to his breast and attempted to appear mystified at his good luck. The game had started with high rollers a good two hours back, but everyone else had washed out and wandered off except for the two of them.

Merle swore and banged his fist on the table hard enough to make the liquor glasses jump and clatter. "That was the last of my pay for three weeks. Now it's back to beans and tortillas at the Double-D tomorrow."

Alec had some sympathy for the dumb rube, despite himself. "Tell you what. The next drink's on me."

Merle frowned and scoffed. "I'd rather kiss a rattlesnake than take your charity."

A sore loser. Not the first Alec had encountered, and definitely not the last.

"Tell you what," Merle attempted. "The real game stakes happen during pinochle time. Give me another chance to win back my greenbacks then, and I'll make you regret you ever stepped into town, you'll be so durned broke."

Alec barely kept his grin from freezing. Pinochle, again? "What a tempting offer. I believe I'll take you up on it at some later date."

Merle left with a sneer.

Alec pocketed his winnings with a stealth born of practice. A little thrill of triumph zinged through him. Having a pocket of bills felt almost as good as a woman's soft skin. Except that $87, while not bad for a regular Wednesday, was more than a bit short of the $4,413 dollars he needed to give Carlene in just two days.

He sipped his brandy and cast his gaze around. The place had uneven floorboards and a rainbow imperfection in the mirror behind the bar. A stand by the door sold cigars and chewing tobacco. Posters of voluptuous beauties revealing bare shoulders and ankles alternated with images of popular pugilists, trick riders, and cavalrymen. A cuckoo clock burst into shrill song every half hour. The cuckoo in question looked more like a mangled raccoon than a bird. The Crystal Palace lacked the classy touches of the Desert Rose, especially the gilding, matching drinkware, and spic and span cleanliness.

As Alec continued his perusal of the saloon, he noticed that despite its name, he could identify neither a crystal nor a palace. Though a glass case filled with some sort of globes did sit in the corner.

A portly gentleman wearing a stained waistcoat approached him. He had slicked-back hair, a bald spot, and avaricious little eyes. "Congratulations, Mr. Malone, on a fine game of poker." He thrust out a pudgy hand. "Beauregard Gleason, at your service."

Alec recognized the name from when he had asked that luscious minx, Texie, about the townspeople. Texie with those dark brown eyes that made his heart beat a little harder. As if she could see right down the middle of him, past all the flash and mirrors, where no one had ever looked before. He took the cretin's hand in order to introduce himself with false heartiness.

Gleason sprayed saliva when he talked. "Indeed, I am delighted to make your acquaintance, Mr. Malone! I see that you are new to town. We need more gentlemen of quality here."

Alec resisted the urge to chuckle. Gleason had as much as called him fresh blood.

"Allow me to show you around my humble establishment."

Alec followed with feigned interest as Gleason pointed out the features of the saloon—the varied kinds of alcohol, the one and only billiards table in the south corner of Southwest Central Texas, the cribs of fancy women out back, and the chicken pasties that the Cornish contingent of town (one whole family's worth) sold on the fourth Tuesday of every other month.

"And these, well, you'll never see anything like these within 200 miles, I guarantee it!"

He led Alec over to the display case and swept his hand out wide, as if introducing the crown jewels or the president of the United States or maybe the ambassador to Saskatchewan. Alec looked close. Glass globes the size of both fists joined together sat on little stands. Liquid filled the hollow interiors of the globes which featured ceramic figures like the Eiffel Tower, the Chartres Cathedral, and . . . was that the Bastille?

"Fantastical, aren't they? Take a look at this." Gleason pulled out a ring of keys from his vest pocket and unlocked the glass doors. He grabbed the globe with the Eiffel Tower in it and shook it. Little white flakes swirled around in the liquid, just like snow.

Alec couldn't help himself. He made an "ooh" of appreciation.

"Here, try it yourself."

Gleason handed over the item, which sat like iron in Alec's hand. Careful not to drop it, he jiggled it himself. Snowflakes drifted around the monument and reminded him of cold winter nights in New York City, perched by the window of his father's library and looking out at the kerosene street lamps that glowed dully in the stillness.

"Straight from France, they are. The only thing around here that is, except for Digger Frou Frou, a lunger who died last year. Snow globes, they are. Or domes, some call them."

Alec shook it again. Little ceramic people surrounded the Eiffel Tower, painted red, black, and yellow. "Well, I'll be damned," he murmured.

Gleason beamed. Three of the globes sat in the center of the cabinet. Crystal figurines of angels, shepherds, and Jesus on the cross sat on the other shelves, along with various likenesses of animals and buildings like the White House. None of them were of particular quality, though.

"These globes are a mite rare," Alec speculated.

"That ain't the half of it. Got them from a special dealer straight from the manufacturer. Why, they are made for finest royal houses in Europe. What a sensation to have them at the Crystal Palace, as well. They're my pride and joy."

"Pricey, I wager."

"You would be bowled over if you knew just how much. But you're not here to talk about my treasures, Mr. Malone, are you?"

"You have a keen understanding of the human animal, Mr. Gleason."

"Indeed. Let me tell you about the keno and faro games we have here on Saturdays. And pinochle, too, should you find that of interest."

Ten minutes of blathering passed before Alec could pry himself from Gleason.

He passed a droopy-eyed, foul-smelling mopper who shuffled among the patrons, hat in hand, as he begged for a sip or two. He was an all-too-recognizable sight in saloons far and wide. Alec tossed him a coin and nodded with a little embarrassment over the man's effusive, "May Jesus and all the saints bless you, gambler!"

Alec strolled down the boardwalk, hand in his pocket and fingers sliding across the treasury bills there. A mighty slim amount of them. Why, if he made $87 a day, he would be able to pay Carlene off in a mere . . . 51 days. Missing her deadline by 49 days was probably too much for her to overlook, even for his considerable persuasive skills.

The door to the telegraph office stood open. A weak, dusty breeze came in off the desert and swirled the stagnant air around a bit. As Alec passed the office, he heard the staccato clicks of the telegraph operator sending a message to some far-off place. The sound reminded him of his neighborhood back in New York and the little cluster of shops, the butcher's, the sweets parlor, the furniture shop, the pawn . . .

The pawn shop.

He snapped his fingers and gave a little laugh of triumph. With a wink at a passing matron, he entered the telegraph office directly.

* * *

The afternoon was warm for a spring day, Texie reflected as she relaxed in a chair on the front porch of the jailhouse. Of course, out here in West Texas, it never got all that cold even at the worst of times. She squinted to the north, where a dust devil whirled high into the sky. The sun shone fiercely through a blue sky utterly devoid of clouds. Underneath, the flat, parched earth sported the occasional mesquite tree and cholla cactus, with some oaks and salt cedars lining the thin winding banks of the Pecos River, but for the most part, the only color out here was unrelentingly brown. She'd grown up climbing over the boulder heaps and running through the dry arroyos, picking prickly pear blossoms and frying agave leaves. Beyond the desert lay the distant outline of the Guadalupe Mountains, jutting and bare. It was a harsh, unforgiving land, and it bred the same type of folks. Herself included, she supposed.

She sipped her lemonade. It was tart enough to pucker her whole face. The general store had been out of sugar for a week now, and she'd used the last of her supply to make this pitcher. Hopefully, a new shipment would come in sometime soon, but such things seemed like surprises more than certainties out here.

She glanced down to the other end of town. Most people were inside, resting during the afternoon. A few stragglers wandered about. An old miner picked at his mule's shoes, and a couple of kids made mud pies in the drippings from the horse trough. Someone exited the stables, valise in hand, and made his way down the main street in her direction. She couldn't make out his face right away. One of these days, she should make the trip over to Albuquerque or El Paso to get some spectacles. As the figure neared, she recognized the familiar, jaunty gait of Alec Malone. She sighed. Of course it was him. When was it ever *not* him lately?

Even in her dreams. Last night, she woke up around

midnight with the image of those smirking, delectable lips emblazoned on her mind. Close enough to touch. But that wasn't all. The crinkles framing his white-blue eyes. The light speckle of neatly-groomed hairs above his ears. Pretty damn fine ears as well. All swirly and whatnot. Ever since she'd been young, she'd noticed people's ears for some strange reason. They fascinated her.

Amos Spartzenhammer's ear swirls had been particularly intriguing. Why, it almost seemed like some gypsy or another should be able to read those swirls and tell you what your future was. If only she'd known the future when first she met Amos. Well, no use thinking about him now. He was long gone in Tennessee or somewhere, raising a passel of kids. The damage he'd done remained, though.

Alec headed into the telegraph office. He seemed to live a disappointingly normal life if the last two days were any indication. He went from the Crystal Palace to the stable where he'd been bedding down after being thrown out of the Desert Rose, to the bathhouse where he presumably divested himself of the horse and goat smell, and to Mrs. Smith's Fixin's for lunch and supper. And now, to the telegraph office to send a message to whatever unfortunate individual talked to the likes of him.

She looked away. Rancho McGillicuddy sat on horseback about fifteen feet in front of her. She jerked in surprise and yelped. "Dang it all, deputy! You know I hate it when you scare me like that."

He gave a laconic shrug. Long silver-white mustachios covered his lips. "Not my fault you have bad hearing."

"I can hear everyone else just fine!"

He scratched the black and white stubble on his neck. The

silver deputy's star on the lapel of his leather vest glinted in the sun. He shifted and dismounted with little more than a tweak of his hips after a lifetime in the saddle. Lanky and weathered, he was hell on wheels in a fight but deliberate and close-lipped the rest of the time. There was no better deputy in six counties.

"What I can't figure out is how you trained your horse to be that quiet. No snorting or nothing."

Ellie Mae was a pretty palomino with ribbons in her mane courtesy of Rancho's granddaughter. Texie got up and scratched under her chin. She whickered and rubbed her big head against Texie's shoulder.

Rancho flicked a scorpion off his pants and watched it scuttle off, pincer high and angry. "Do you want to hear what I have to say or go on railing against me?"

"I'm listening."

"'Bout time."

He took off his hat to smooth down the wiry mess he called hair and then replaced it so it sat back further on his head, revealing more of his face. "The rumors are true. They're back. Hiding out somewhere in the Guadalupes."

She took a long blink. "I guess you're sure about that."

His craggy brown face didn't register annoyance. He squinted down the street. "Yup. I found a bunch of tracks over near the crossroads at the Arroyo and the Butterfield Route. A couple of vaqueros said a party of horsemen came through a few weeks ago, whooping and hollering and stampeding their herd all to hell. The leader was a skinny old feller who wore a sombrero and cussed up a storm."

"Sounds like them. Damn it."

She'd chased the Bully Flamenco gang out of the territory

just last summer and they were already back. Her back itched. She could not abide a bunch of rotten, stinking thieves and murderers in her county. It wouldn't be easy finding them in the endless caves and defiles of the Guadalupes, though.

Alec exited the telegraph office and lifted a hand in acknowledgement to her before striding right into the Desert Rose. The expected screams of bloody murder from Carlene did not materialize.

Since that man stepped off the stage, things had gotten worse and worse, what with trying to figure out his sneaky plans and now this. She couldn't help but wonder if he'd brought an ill wind with him.

Chapter 6

Texie was refrying a skillet of mashed-up pinto beans when she glanced out her kitchen window. It was about eight pm and pitch dark, except over to the east where an orange glow caught her eye. The moon got pretty big every now and again, and that's what it must be. She set the skillet aside and strode out the front door, expecting to take a gander at a downright romantical sight before finishing up her dinner. Instead, she gawked, cursed, and took off running toward the Crystal Palace.

"Fire brigade!" she hollered. "Get out the fire brigade!"

Someone who sounded like Ellie Mae Fleetwood screamed to high heaven. A couple of dogs set to barking. Townspeople boiled out of buildings. Some stood still in surprise while others ran this way and that. The church bell shrilled out quick, desperate clangs.

Smoke puffed out the saloon's front door and side windows like a gentleman enjoying an evening cigar. Flames roared from the upstairs chimneys like the fires of hell. On the leeward side of the building, a few of the soiled doves clung together, half-dressed and disheveled. One of them was crying.

Texie headed for them and barked in her no-nonsense law-woman's voice, "Is everyone out of the building?"

A dry-eyed redhead by the name of Shilly McGill answered, "No, but they're coming. Everyone's down from the second floor."

"What about that one man—the crazy one?" piped in a skinny thing about as tall as a half-grown boy. "I saw him run back in there!"

"Me, too. I don't think he's come out."

Everyone seemed to be in agreement about that fact.

"Aw, hell," Texie muttered.

Little Jimmy Fleetwood dragged a heavy bucket of water over. Texie grabbed it, doused her bandanna, then dumped the rest of it over her head.

"If I don't come back out in ten minutes or so, you'll have to get yourselves a new sheriff." The bystanders watched her with all the comprehension of pigs at a philosophical lecture.

She tied the bandanna over her nose and mouth and ran toward the building. At the batwing doors, she dodged a couple of old farts stumbling out, hacking. One clutched his beer to his chest like an infant. Inside, the gas lights on the walls still burned with dim persistence, but they did little to penetrate the smoke-filled interior. She bent low and searched the floor for legs other than those of the chairs.

Just when she'd about decided that the crazy fellow had slipped out the back way, she tripped over a lump on the floor. She landed hard on her hip on a man-like surface.

"You trying to kill me?" Croaked a voice that dissolved into wracking coughs.

She felt around until she was able to grab a part of the fellow that allowed her some purchase. A yank and a shove didn't do anything to move him, so she rolled back on her fanny with her back against a wall and positioned her booted feet on what she presumed, from the feel of it, was an ass. She thrust her legs with all her strength.

Like a newborn calf taking his first steps, the shove pushed the man to his knees. Another one brought him up to his feet. He staggered toward what she hoped was the door. A loud thump and a hoarse curse told her that he'd found the wall instead. It was easy to do in the featureless gray. She tried to think straight. Now was not the time to run around like a horse with his tail on fire.

The sounds of the crowd seemed louder to the right. She lurched to her feet and aimed in the general direction of the dimwit. Luck favored her, and she managed to hook an arm around his elbow and steer them toward the saloon doors. She hit the side hinges with her left shoulder and heard another thump as her charge hit the wall again. Her right shoulder did not meet with resistance. Thank the Lord!

She barreled out the door, tugging the unfortunate man along. They both stepped wrong over the edge of the boardwalk and lost their footing. She sprawled, and *splash*, landed on her bottom on the muddy street. The man landed on top of her—a solid *whoof* and dead weight. His chest lay on hers. One of his arms flopped to the left of her, and he groped around until he found the dark shape of a valise. Texie flailed like a bug trapped under a child's thumb.

It took a moment before he stirred to consciousness. As he did, a questing hand found her right breast—the one she secretly thought of as her best one. Despite its merits, she didn't want it molested. She yelped as he squeezed and made a *mmm* noise.

"Get your dad-blasted paws off me!" She wheezed and punctuated her words with an awkward knee to his crotch.

All that wiggling around roused him further. He nuzzled her neck and slipped a questing knee between her legs.

"Mary Mae?"

When his head came up, she tightened her neck muscles and slammed her forehead into his nose with all her strength. A blast of pain at her hairline told her that it connected pretty well.

An agonized groan preceded his rolling off her. He landed on his side, his back propped up against the valise. The dim light revealed the sharp edge of his jaw.

She sat up. "Malone?"

He blinked and his eyes cleared. Then his face creased into a grimace and he moaned and coughed again. He looked at her out of the corner of his eye. "At your" —*choke, gasp*— "service, Sheriff."

She scrambled to her knees, then her feet. It took a mighty effort to resist the urge to boot him where he lay. Of all the folks in town who deserved to be rescued from the conflagration, she had to go and pluck this degenerate out of it. He felt around for the valise beside him. The action annoyed her to a considerable degree.

"You couldn't have left that behind?"

"It's got all my money in it. So no way in" —he coughed for a few minutes— "hell."

Everyone else was running around, calling for water and hooking up the brand-new fire hose that came direct from Chicago, Illinois. She knew she should get up and help them, but her legs felt rubbery and she kept coughing up smoke.

Right about then, someone ran up and led her over to the boardwalk on the other side of the street. She sat down hard, dizzy all of a sudden. That same someone left for a few minutes and returned to put a cool cloth over her sore, abused eyes. Ah. That felt good.

A great roar of delight accompanied a gush of water out of the fire hose. A half-dozen local men maneuvered the contraption around. The source of the fire seemed to come from the back of the saloon where the stove sat. It figured. That's where they usually started.

They managed to drown the flames after a bit, enough for a few men with bandanas covering their mouths to get in there with axes and take out the hot spots that remained. She sat and watched them for a good hour or two.

When she thought to look up again, Alec had disappeared along with his damned valise.

* * *

By the time Texie made it back to her kitchen, the kerosene lamp had guttered out and her refried beans were burned to gravel-sized nubs. She tossed the pan in the bucket of water she kept for dirty dishes. It sizzled and steam flooded up. She was lucky her kitchen hadn't caught on fire.

"Nice place, if a little dark." A rough voice spoke from the doorway.

Alec. His lean outline, complete with hat, stood framed at the door, which she had unwisely left unlatched. She rummaged around the cupboard for the matches.

"Oh, it's you." She tried not to sound too disappointed. Whenever possible, she tried not to be rude. She really did. "No lasting effect from your little adventure?"

The flare of lamplight illuminated his head shake and shrug. "It appears not. Guess I was lucky the sheriff pulled me out of there."

"You wanna tell me what you were doing there in the saloon at that hour, anyhow?"

He shrugged, drawing her attention to the fine cut of his shoulder. He'd apparently gone straight to the washbasin to clean up. "You know me. Always up for a roll in the hay. Or crib, as the case may be."

Something about his expression didn't read right.

She looked at him. "How about the truth this time?"

"So maybe I wanted a nightcap but the bar was closed. And maybe I figured I'd go in there and help myself—leaving my money on the bar like a law-abiding citizen—when this gigantic lug of a night watchman attacked me. Naturally, I defended myself. Sometime in the midst of his unconscious descent to the floor, he upset one of the kerosene lamps."

"Wait. Are you telling me that *you* started the fire?"

He looked sheepish. "In a roundabout, entirely innocent, purely accidental manner. Without admitting to any fault of my own and blaming it on that overzealous Irish mountain of a fellow. I did drag him to safety, I'd like to point out. But in doing so, I left my valise inside, and well, you know what happened after that."

His tone brought to mind their bodies touching, as if she had been able to stop thinking about it. He moved closer. She never seemed to notice his height unless he was standing alongside her. Why was it that he filled up her senses and disturbed her more than the dozens of outlaws she'd confronted over the last couple of years? She needed a diversion, and quickly. Her voice sounded like rusty forks across a chalkboard. "What do you want?"

"To convey my sincere appreciation. If you hadn't tossed

me out of there . . . well, it's best not to dwell on might-have-beens, especially when they are so dismal. Would you allow me to give you a token of my appreciation?"

She snorted. "I don't need no token—"

One graceful stride brought him in front of her. She took a step back, startled. He followed her, standing far too close. A rush of heat seared her face.

"I beg to differ."

"What are you doing?" It came out softer and far less strident than she had anticipated.

"Giving you something else."

She blew out an exasperated breath. "You gave my teat a good grab. That was enough."

He grinned. "As nice as that was—and believe me, Texie, it was *incredibly* nice—it was also wrong of me to molest your person in such a manner. And afterward, when I thought you were Mary Mae, that insatiable Boston beauty I used to know . . . my only excuse is smoke dementia. Please, accept my apology."

This close, she could smell his musky scent, smoke and spices. He leaned in and she held her breath, suddenly paralyzed. Her palms itched. They wanted to crawl up his back. She concentrated on keeping them flat against the wooden tabletop. His lips were so close that . . . glory, hallelujah. She felt her own lips part. They remained untouched as he pressed a moist kiss to her cheek, accompanied by a faint scrape of razor stubble.

He tilted his head to look her in the eyes, still far too close. Embarrassment made her cheeks hot. She swallowed and collected herself.

"Yeah, yeah. You're forgiven and whatever. Now stand back,

will you? Your breath smells like an ashtray."

His lips twitched and he raised one eyebrow. She tried to scoot out around him but he put out a hand to stop her. Not forcefully. Just a gentle barrier of muscle and intention.

His voice dropped lower. "What is it, Texie? Am I making you nervous?"

She summoned up a bucketful of indignation. "No, you lunkhead. You're making me impatient. Now get out of here before I crack you over the head with Ole Hank." She gestured to Hank, who leaned against the wall in his regular spot next to the coat hanger and the gun belt which holstered her Colt, Miss Jennie.

Alec drew back to take her in from shoe to skull. He whistled. "I *am* making you uncomfortable. Well, I'll be damned. It's a peculiar feeling, but I think I like it."

He moved to the doorway where he paused. With a flick of a finger, he tipped his hat. "Evening, sugar plum. I'll be seeing you around."

The sound of his footsteps disappeared as he stepped off the porch. For the second time that night, sudden weakness overcame her. She felt around for the chair and sagged into it. Her heart thudded like railroad men hammering down spikes. She lifted her hand and saw that it was shaking.

Either the smoke and flames had gotten to her more than she thought or that dodgasted snake in the grass had gone and done something to her.

Nah. No chance of that.

It was the smoke all the way.

Chapter 7

A lec stumbled across the rocky earth, heavy valise tucked under his arm as the long rays of the sunrise spread like gold paint across the desert floor. Birds had not even awakened yet, but movement in the sagebrush revealed a coyote, ears pricked to attention. The animal's mottled tan coat blended in almost completely with the dried-out surroundings. An old-timer had told Alec that coyotes sometimes ran in packs. If they got hungry enough, people might be on the menu. Alec patted his jacket pocket, checking to make sure his one and only weapon, a Swiss knife he'd taken in trade during a faro game, was there. It was. Not that it would do much good on account of the fact that the blade was four inches long. The can opener, though. That might be lethal.

"Git!" Alec yelled.

The coyote obliged, tucking tail and melting into the brush.

Alec straightened his shoulders. *That's right, you scalawag. You should be afraid.*

He turned his attention back to searching for the perfect landmarks. He considered, and then dismissed, this truly impressive clump of prickly pear and that creosote flat. But those two immense boulders that leaned against one another like drunkards on their way home . . . they just might work. Especially when he noticed a hollow between them that looked like the perfect shape and size for his burden.

Alec tossed his valise down with a solid *thwap*. He cringed, then opened the case to check on the two snow globes within. Like a clumsy moron, he'd knocked the Eiffel Tower globe over back in the saloon and it smashed to bits on the floor.

Well, the night before last hadn't turned out too bad in the end. He got the snow globes, didn't die in the fire, and succeeded in ruffling Sheriff Texie's pretty, prickly feathers. That woman's tongue might be as venomous as a scorpion's sting, but she was sure soft in all the right places. He smiled at the memory.

Alec found a stick and poked it into the rock opening. When a rattlesnake or gila monster didn't fling itself at him, fangs bared, he stuck his hands inside and cleared out enough rocks to make a nice little niche for his treasures. He fished the precious globes out of his valise and placed them inside, wrapped in his extra clothes. He crammed brush in the hole and piled some rocks outside, then admired his handiwork. Hopefully, the hiding place would be safe enough from wind storms, flash floods, and lightning strikes.

As soon as he could arrange for transportation back to New York city and his trusty fence, Armor Blankenship, without arousing undue suspicion from the town yahoos, he would. Armor had been good enough to advance him $3,000 for the sale. Between that and the fifteen hundred-odd dollars he'd earned at an all-night pinochle tournament prior to burning up his place of employment, he had met Carlene's demands with seven minutes to spare. She made a show of counting out every last dollar before saying, "Orange lollipop."

"Pardon?"

"That's Snarly Pete's password. If you don't get it right, he'll blast a hole in your head the size of a watermelon."

"Oh. Well, then, thank you. As for his location?"

She shrugged a pretty chiffon shoulder. "I'm sure I don't know. Probably holed up somewhere nice and secluded until he and his gang run out of money or ditch the federales."

"But—"

"Give yourself some credit, Mr. Malone. I'm sure you'll find him. Eventually. And when you do, you can give him my regards. Now, in light of recent incendiary events, I have a mandatory fire evacuation plan to go over with my employees. Good day to you."

Alec considered further persuasion but decided that he would leave that for another time. On the way out the door, Mary Ann, dustpan and broom in hand, smiled and winked at him. He nodded but ran outside like a scalded hog before he could get himself in another mess like the last one.

Now, with a satisfied sigh, he stood up to kick some dirt over his footprints. Valise tucked back under his arm, he began making his way back to town. That's when movement and a flash of long, shiny, dark hair caught his eye. He leapt like a jackrabbit behind a spindly creosote bush and ducked down. His heart struck against his chest in a rapid *tat-tat-tat*.

Indians!

He'd heard far too many tales of white folks being scalped, burned at the stake, and in general, gleefully stabbed to feel great about meeting Indians unawares. He peered through the brush at the figure.

One person moved in a light-footed but not completely silent manner. A tan Mexican hat with a pinched crown sat atop his head and a stick rested across his shoulders. Alec squinted.

"I'll be a flibberty gibbet."

Not a man after all but a woman. And not just any woman. Texie. Now what in the six hells was she doing out here at this time of the morning?

His plan had been to get back to town as soon as possible and set about replenishing the rather anemic state of his finances. But this . . . this intrigued him. The nicely endowed sheriff seemed to be up to something suspicious. What other reason could she have for being out here at this hour?

He waited until she had nearly passed out of sight and crept after her as quietly as he could. After half an hour of picking his way across the desert floor, avoiding boot heels on rocks and the scraping of clothing against stickers and brush—all the while trying to keep Texie in sight—he had to stop and rest for a minute or two. He squeezed his eyes shut to ease the burning caused by the bright sun.

When he finished blinking enough to moisten his peepers, he located Texie's tan hat among the brush. Right there, about forty-five degrees west from his current position and fifty or so yards from him.

Then she jerked to a halt. She sniffed the wind. He'd spent the last few days burping up a spicy sausage he'd been gnawing on whenever he didn't feel like eating at Mama Carmen's. Surely, she couldn't smell that. No, probably a skunk or something.

She whip-cracked around like a trick shooter, revolver out and pointed right at his head. He gulped. She strode toward him, the sights of her six gun never wavering from the tip of his nose. As he watched the hollow barrel come closer, his eyes crossed.

"You!"

She took her thumb off the hammer and reholstered the gun. Her left hand gripped Ole Hank like she was ready to swing it upside his head.

"You're following me?" She sounded outraged.

He tried to charm her with a grin. "Would you be flattered if I said yes?"

"Not especially. I am out here on official business. You need to go back to town right now, Mister."

"Official business. Is that so? Where's your horse?"

"Back in town. I don't use her when I—I mean, I like to walk when I'm doing my business. So to speak."

He snickered.

She looked less than amused. "What are you doing out at this hour of the morning? I figured you slept until long about 10 am most days. And why do you have that stupid valise with you?"

The next thing he knew, she had snatched it from under his arm. She flipped it open and pawed through his extra shirt, small clothes, pens, scraps of paper, address book, and shaving blade. When she got to his jockstrap, she dangled it in the air and looked at him with a question in her eyes. He didn't suppose they had such equipment out here. She shoved it back in the bag and pulled out his small wooden box. She popped it open.

He contrived to look the other way.

"What are these?"

She held up the long cylindrical-shaped rubbers. The morning sun made them transparent.

"And what's this for?" She plucked up the little jar of petroleum jelly associated with the rubbers.

Her face wrinkled as understanding dawned. She dropped the items like they were hot coals and slammed the lid back on the box. Then she turned her head and pressed a hand to her mouth in a maidenly gesture, the first one he'd ever seen her make.

Her voice was a little high. "I don't know why I'm surprised."

"I aim to be prepared for female attentions whenever and wherever I might find them. Even when I'm out for my morning constitutional."

She slid her gaze back to him. "Don't get any ideas. You ain't gonna use those with me."

He lowered his voice and quirked an eyebrow. "You sure? I could show you a good time."

Her cheeks flamed. "No! And you know what? Just get out of here. Right now. I told you I have things to do."

She turned and headed back the way she'd come, walking fast.

He hurried after her. "Now, Miss Texie, I am worried about you. A woman alone in the Great American Desert, surrounded by buzzards and wild Indians and lust-crazed cowhands."

She scowled at him. "I can handle myself just fine."

"I know you don't think much of me, Sheriff, but I aim to behave like a gentleman at least a quarter of the time I'm awake. When I saw you headed out here all reckless-like, I just didn't feel right about letting you go. And being aware of your penchant for . . . disagreeable notions regarding me, I decided to follow you unawares."

She stopped and regarded him with flattened lips. A fisted hand rested on her hip. "I wish I could believe a word out of your mouth. Just one single word."

He drew back in surprise. He had no idea how to respond to that.

She scratched the end of her nose. "Look, the truth is that I don't need no tenderfoot like you distracting me while I do what I mean to do."

"My chivalrous instincts just won't allow that, I'm afraid."

"Goodbye, Mr. Malone." She turned her back on him.

He watched her go for a few moments. Clearly, she didn't want his assistance. And if he was honest with himself—which he rarely was—she didn't need it either. But there was something so . . . irresistible about her. He had sensed it from the first time he'd seen her. He did what he always did when faced with a choice—he went with what thrilled him the most.

He followed her. And after copious sweet-talking and resolute pursuit on his part, she gave a resigned sigh and let him.

* * *

A good three hours later, they came upon an abandoned rock dwelling. The stick and mud roof had caved in some time ago and the front door hung half off its hinges. Texie walked in like she owned the place and sank down against a wall with a groan. With a tinny clank, she unscrewed the lid of her canteen and took a swig of water.

Alec dropped next to her and immediately tore off his boots. The damn things looked good, but they were not designed for long-distance tramping across the desert. He pulled off his socks and examined the sores on the outer edges of his feet.

"Oooooh eeee." Texie fanned the air under her nose. "Did

you have to do that right next to me?"

"My apologies, darling," he drawled. "I wouldn't have done it if I wasn't in particular discomfort."

"If that's the case, you could turn around and head back," she suggested for the eighteenth time.

He considered her. Lord, but she looked beautiful with a little flush to her cheeks and newly moistened lips. He had to stop himself from imagining kissing those lips for real this time.

"You're awfully eager to get rid of me. I wonder why."

She looked out the window at the cloud-scudded sky, then exhaled in defeat. "If you must know, I am tracking down the Bully Flamenco gang. I reckon they're holed up in the mountains hereabouts. Leastways, that's where I would hide if I were part of a gang of murderin', thievin' cattle rustlers and counterfeiters."

"The Bully Flamenco gang!" he blurted out. Why, just the fellows he was after! What luck. He reined in his perhaps-too-enthusiastic reaction. "But that's dangerous. I don't care how good you are with that revolver, you don't stand a chance against upwards of forty hardened criminals."

She handed him the canteen. He gulped a couple of swallows of tepid but refreshing water.

"Relax, Malone. I'm just out here scouting. Nothing else for now."

"That does salve my manly concern a mite. But it makes me even more determined to accompany you. Despite my own considerable agony."

He picked at his injuries more. She watched him fuss for a while, her lips slightly crooked in amusement, before getting up.

"Wait here."

She went outside for a few breaths. When she returned, she thrust a handful of light grayish-greenish leaves at him. He ran his thumb over them. Soft.

"The Indians use them in their papooses' wraps to soak up messes. Put 'em in your boots. They'll help."

He followed her suggestion, then pulled his boots on gingerly. After walking a few steps hither and thither to try them out, he exclaimed, "I'll be. My unbearable agony is much improved. Thank you." He took her hand. "That's a kind gesture."

She pulled her hand away and ducked her head in uncharacteristically maidenly embarrassment. *"De nada."*

He smiled at her and swayed in her direction.

She grabbed Ole Hank up and jabbed it toward him. "Don't go getting too familiar."

He backed off.

She threw him a warning look and stalked out the door. He took to habit and scurried after her.

* * *

By mid-afternoon, Texie's pace had slowed to a plod and they had not gotten one iota closer to the stark, looming mountains that seemed to be her destination. The side of Alec's feet no longer hurt. Now it was the arches, a dull, consistent ache that made him feel like an abused, unshod mule. He tried not to think about the permanent damage he was doing to himself. A distraction, that's what he needed. Since his favorite distraction—bed bouncing with a willing partner—was out of the question, he turned to his second-favorite distraction, conversating.

"Miss Texie, I find myself powerfully curious about what sort of upbringing leads a young girl to take up after her daddy in the law-enforcing trade."

She gave him a sideways glance under the brim of her hat. "Is that your long-winded way of asking about my youth?"

"I would dispute that it is a perfectly winded approach, but yes, you could say that."

She snorted. "You're a piece of work, Malone. I've got to give you that."

He beamed at her. "I'll take whatever you're giving out, darling."

She grumbled a bit. "I don't know. What do you want me to say? I was born and raised in Abalone. Plan on being here until I meet the Good Lord and Jesus both. Although I have heard tell of San Francisco. It seems like such a fantastical place that I'd like to see it some time."

"San-Fran-cisco." He let the name draw out on his tongue. "I've heard tales of it, too. Running wild with faro and poker and dancing women and happy go-lucky gold miners. It does sound like paradise on earth, I agree."

"I don't think we define paradise in the same way."

"True." He considered her. "I hope this isn't your way of avoiding my question."

She ducked her head and kicked a rock in her path.

"Come on now, beautiful. We've got all the time in the world. I'm a good listener, among other things."

He waggled his eyebrows at her. She rolled her eyes.

"Hate to disappoint you, but there's not a whole lot to tell. Papa came west from Missouri. He met my Ma on the train and fell in love with her the first time he set eyes on her. I can't blame him none. She was a looker." Texie straightened up and adjusted her breasts. "My bosoms came from her."

Alec felt his jaw drop. A bit of drool may have dripped out. He swiped a hand across his chin to save himself from her notice. She noticed anyhow and gave a single happy bark of laughter.

"You are one randy goat of a man, Alec Malone. Yes, indeed."

"In my defense, you do make it hard for a fellow to control himself."

"I like to think that my bosoms are all that I inherited from that woman. She never did like Abalone that much. Said it was full of shit kickers and malcontents. My daddy did everything he knew of to make her happy—even sent away to Kansas City for a china cabinet and new fancy dishes. Back then, he had a bit of coin on account of selling land plots. He joined with a bunch of investors who had a mind to create the perfect town out in Colorado. They called it Miller's Well. That's a nice name, isn't it? It didn't matter. The Plains Indians were fighting settlers all over the place, and no one wanted to risk an arrow through the throat so the town went bust. Ma ran off after that. Just kind of gave up on Papa, and me, too. That's when I ripped up all my skirts and set fire to the new ones Papa tried to get me to wear. Ma died a few years later—fever, we think—and Papa never did get over it."

"She couldn't have been all that bad. She raised up a right fine daughter."

A shadow of a grin hung about the edge of her lips. "Flatterer."

An unexpected silence made him scramble to fill it. "I suppose it is my turn, now. My mama was a damn fine woman. She was the fastest auctioneer in Manhattan. Taught me how to call out auctions faster than any kid in the fashion district—when she wasn't dancing the can-can on Broadway, that is."

"She . . . what?"

"Nah, just teasing. I can whip up a good story when I want to, can't I?"

"I suppose you can. Now will you kindly shut up? Voices carry out here, and I don't want to walk back with a whole lot of nothing because you couldn't stop airing your teeth out."

Now that affronted him some. Not that he let it show. "Whatever you want, darling. I'm obliging, I am."

"And stop admiring my bosoms."

He didn't comply with that request. Some things were just beyond his earthly control.

Chapter 8

Alec didn't usually second-guess his decisions. He believed in running full-bore after whatever enterprise seemed like a good idea at the time. However, as the afternoon light began to lengthen and turn golden and they continued on across the sand-blasted desert, Alec began to regret following Texie, no matter that he appreciated the view of her derriere. His stomach was growling like a bear with a thorn in his foot.

Texie stopped in front of a twisted, stunted pine tree and plucked a handful of pebble-sized nuts off the branches. She handed them to him.

He eyed them. "Poison is against your moral convictions, I hope."

"Usually. Eat them. They're pinyon nuts. Delicious when you're starving."

She didn't lie. They tasted as good as fresh-roasted chestnuts. He made appreciative noises and savored every little nugget.

She peered into the distance. When she spoke, her voice was offhanded. "I must confess to some curiosity about your arrival in Abalone, Malone."

"I, my dear lady, am a rolling stone. I gather no moss and I like it that way. There's a whole world out there, and I aim to see it sooner or later. And gold is calling to me. Why, can you imagine just how much of it is lying under the rocks out yonder? Pounds and pounds. Tons, even!"

"You mean to tell me that a dandy like yourself is gonna put spade to soil?"

"Certainly not. I will eye the land and plot out the most likely strike locations. Then I will hire a few poor fools to dig it up for me."

"I should have known."

They walked on quietly for a bit more. Then she said carefully, "Doesn't that get old after a while? Never knowing anybody, always learning a new place? I think I'd feel . . . I don't know the word exactly."

"Lonely? Sometimes, I reckon. I find that the blessing of female companionship alleviates that particular emotion *tout de suite.*"

"Yes, it would. So you'll be heading out afore long, huh? Once you find out there ain't no gold around here."

He couldn't tell if she sounded hopeful or not. "I have to ponder on that. Summer's coming, and I'm not much of one for traveling when the countryside is broiling."

She snorted in amusement. "Then you'll be staying in Abalone, I reckon. The summer will be here before you know it, and desert is every which way you go in this area."

"I've found stifling heat to be much more bearable in the saloon with a bottle of whisky to the right of me and a freshly shuffled deck of cards to the left."

She stopped and squinted at the horizon.

"What do you know? Looks like someone took up residence at the old Smith homestead."

He peered at the unbroken countryside where he saw

nothing but dirt and a bunch of scraggly bushes.

"Come along, then." She strode toward this mythical place. "I can smell corn pone and beans from here."

The Old Smith homestead was a half-broken adobe affair with a roof made of dried ocotillo branches and clapboard that must have fallen off some pioneer's prairie schooner fifty years ago. A dozen or so chickens pecked around the feet of a donkey and a cow in a makeshift corral on one side, and on the other side sat rows of freshly turned soil dotted with corn seedlings.

Just as they approached, a squat, Indian-dark woman bustled out the front door carrying a bucket of corn husks. She froze when she saw them and her eyes widened like those of a wall-eyed mare. Over her shoulder, she cried, "Ernesto!"

Texie burst out with a soothing stream of Spanish, the meaning of which completely eluded Alec. A man who looked remarkably similar to the woman sprang out the door with a carbine pointed at them.

Alec let out a sound akin to that of a rabbit lunged at by a rattlesnake. He thrust his hands into the air. Texie explained their presence in rapid Spanish. At least he hoped that's what she was doing. After a few moments, the couple relaxed and lowered the gun. They came out to greet them.

"This is Consuela and her husband, Ernesto," Texie told him.

He nodded at them both and shook their hands with a vigor borne of relief. After which he bowed slightly to Consuela, who giggled at the formality.

"Hello," Ernesto said to him in heavily accented English.

A lot of incomprehensible talk ensued, along with compli-cated gestures, smiles, and head bows. The couple ushered them inside their tiny, cramped hovel. A single feather bed sat in the middle of the room, covered with Mexican blankets. The adobe walls had been newly patched, and straw and little rocks textured the walls. An altar with freshly picked wildflowers and a hand-drawn picture of the Virgin Mary took up space by the rough-hewn door. The only other furniture was a small chest and a skinny table made out of a slab of lumber and four rickety supports.

Consuela led Texie over to the smoldering fire in the corner and chattered while they stirred a pot of beans and dug tamales out of the ashes.

Ernesto pointed out a bucket of water in the corner and made the motion of splashing water over his face. Alec took the hint and washed his hands and face.

Before long, they sat on braided rugs on the floor, tamales and beans on two dishes between them. Alec restrained himself from moaning too loudly at the opportunity to fill his shrunken belly, especially after Texie elbowed him in the side. He ignored the tiny gray mouse that zipped across the room halfway through dinner.

After the meal, Ernesto broke out a bottle of some sort of fermented agave juice, from which they all took swallows. Texie entertained them with a long stream of incomprehensible conversation. Alec could make out the word "gringo" several times. The laughter that followed made him certain she was talking about him.

Alec took his retribution soon enough when Ernesto pointed from Texie to him. "You marry?"

Texie laughed, high and disbelieving.

"*Si,*" Alec burst out. He slid his arms around Texie's waist and hugged her close before she could grab Ole Hank and smash his head in. "*Muy, muy amor.*" He puckered up for a kiss.

She shoved him back. He spilled onto his backside.

"Rawr," he growled, making his fingers into cat claws.

Ernesto hooted with laughter and Consuela tittered. Texie shot daggers at him with her eyes. She spoke in Spanish again, this time making gestures at Alec, one of which involved flipping her palm upward rigidly and then allowing it to flop over, limp. Consuela went wall-eyed again, but this time the laughter sounded awkward. Texie regarded him with smug satisfaction, and Alec decided to refrain from further teasing to retain what little remained of his dignity.

The sun set and distant coyotes yipped greetings to one another. After a few more swallows of potent swill and some hilarious conversation the likes of which left Alec completely in the dark, Consuela yawned and nudged Ernesto. He nodded, and they shuffled around, putting up the remaining food and gathering a couple of serapes from the corner.

Ernesto gestured at the bed and told Texie something along the lines of, "Take our bed for the night."

"No, we couldn't possibly!" Texie cried out, panicked enough to resort to English.

Rapid, demanding Spanish followed as the two of them shooed Texie and Alec toward the bed.

"Come on, sweet potato," Alec urged. "We need to remedy that little *problem* of mine, don't we?"

Texie cursed under her breath like a particularly foul-mouthed sailor.

Ernesto chuffed and said something that got him a whack in the arm from Consuela. Then they were out the door to the lean-to in the back to slumber alongside the farm animals.

Alec held up his hands in surrender. "I know what you're thinking. I was merely trying to uphold our disguises in the interests of law and order."

In the quiet that followed, Texie allowed, "They were getting offended that we might not accept their hospitality."

Alec toed off his boots and stripped off his vest. Texie swallowed, her face still. He chuckled and flopped onto the bed, palms resting under his skull and elbows crooked wide. She searched around the pile of tools and debris under the table.

"What's the matter, darlin'? You never been in bed with a fine specimen of a man like me? I'll be gentle and sweet, I promise."

"You'll be stabbed and skewered if you try anything."

"Far be it for me to impugn your honor, my lady. Now, come to bed." He winked and leered.

She grumbled something uncomplimentary about his ancestry, but before long, she sat down on the edge of the bed. A weight fell between them. He looked over to see that she'd positioned Ole Hank down the middle of the bed to divide them.

"Aw, now don't do that."

"It's going to stay there unless you want to sleep in the dirt over there by the door."

That certainly wasn't going to happen. He sighed in surrender.

She fiddled around, taking off her boots and bandanas and removing the handful of bullets secreted in the pocket over her left breast and at her hip. When she finally lay down, it was on her back, stiff as Ole Hank and as far to the edge of the bed as she could possibly manage.

He glanced over at her. "Now, you know I'm teasing you. When we finally do get in bed together, you are going to do it willingly. Why, I venture to say that you will be begging me for it."

She returned his glance. "You must be dreaming already, because I'd sooner bed down with four scorpions and a passel of roadrunners. Six days of the week and Sunday all year long."

He smirked. "Methinks the lady doth protest too much. It's all right. I can be patient when I need to be. Good night, my pretty. Sleep well."

She huffed and shut up.

The fire burned down to coals, and moonlight glowed around the gaps in the smoke pipe stuck in the ceiling. At last, Texie turned on her side, the curve of a hip and long hair over one shoulder apparent. Something twisted in the vicinity of his chest. Indigestion, undoubtedly.

He lay awake a long time after her breath went deep and regular before he, too, fell asleep.

Chapter 9

Texie woke with sunrise the next morning, like usual. Outside, she heard the chickens clucking and Consuela talking to them in Spanish like they were her children.

"No, little one, let Mama go first. Juanita, move over. No pecking! Ah, Mama. Good eggs today. Very good!"

At that moment, it occurred to Texie that a warm hand was cradling hers. That brought her to full consciousness instantly.

Alec slept on his side facing her, lips parted and arm thrown over Ole Hank, who apparently did little to separate them. His hand was big and sun-browned, the nails neatly cut straight across. So . . . male compared to her own small hand and thin fingers. She snatched her hand away.

Alec roused with a confused, "Huh?"

When he saw her, a sleepy smile curved his lips. He patted her shoulder. "Come on, strawberry jam, let's sleep a little longer."

The blanket molded around his groin. It showed a hard ridge right about the location of his pecker.

"What is that all about?" she screeched and jabbed a finger in its general direction.

He squinted down at himself. "Err . . . yes, of course. It's perfectly natural in the morning. You seem interested . . ."

"Interested in keeping it away from me."

His eyes lit up in that way they did when he was hassling her. She'd come to recognize it. "You never saw one of those before? Up close, I mean."

"Of course I have. On horses and dogs and whatnot."

"Not on a real live man, though. A close, interested, willing fellow." His voice fell low and husky. "Want to touch it?"

She surged off the bed—not an easy task since it only sat about a foot and a half off the dirt floor. "No, you reprobate. Emphatically no."

He raised himself up on an elbow. "Why, Miss Texie Cortez. Don't tell me that a fine young filly like you has never been a courtin'. And feelin' around—"

"Well, yeah."

She thought back to the smelly cowhands and leering old miners, and further back, when she was sixteen or so. There had been one particular teenaged bronco buster who cornered her after the summer hoe-down and kissed her like her lips tasted of cherry pie. Others had shown interest, too, and she'd even reciprocated a few times.

"I have been engaged twice. Once for serious, even," she informed him primly.

"That's it? You're what? Twenty-six, twenty-seven? And as gorgeous as they come." He sounded incredulous.

"Twenty-five, and I don't want to talk about it."

He considered her like he didn't know quite what to make of her. He was going to push it. She knew he was.

"All right. We don't have to."

Would he ever stop surprising her? Probably about the same time he stopped annoying and aggravating her.

So, long about never, then.

Breakfast consisted of tortillas and honey and strong black coffee. Afterward, Texie questioned Ernesto about what he'd seen thereabouts. Riders and bad hombres and whatnot. He didn't know much, except that he heard hooting and hollering one night and had found hoof prints another couple of times, leading up into the hills.

She warned him about outlaws, and he pointed to the hook on the wall that held his gun belt and revolver. His old US Cavalry-issued Springfield Trapdoor carbine leaned up against the wall next to it. Consuela held up her cast iron skillet with a wicked gleam in her eye.

In Spanish, Consuela urged her to stay. "There are so few women in this place. My sisters are over the border and I miss them so."

"I wish I could." Texie meant her words. But duty called.

Alec thanked them for their hospitality and gave Ernesto his other shirt, a bleached white thing with crisp collars more fit for a dancing hall than a dirt farm. Still, Ernesto beamed when he saw it. Texie took off her relatively new bandanna and gave it to Consuela, along with a leather sack of pinyon nuts she'd collected yesterday (while grumbling that Alec had used up her food supplies since she'd only brought enough for herself).

The couple stood arm in arm, watching them as they headed out.

"So, where are we off to this fine morning?" Alec asked. He seemed to be in a cheerful mood. His eyes sparkled and his tongue wagged.

"Up yonder." She pointed to low rolling hills and the canyon between them where green pines and juniper sprouted half-size and stubby. The trees got bigger the higher into the mountains they went. "As far as I can tell."

He squinted at her. "You don't know?"

"Not really. This is a scouting expedition. It's where I would hole up, if I were them. Fresh water, good access from the road, and lots of caves and blind turns and other places to hide."

"Makes sense."

Off they went. The tortillas they had for breakfast wore off around mid-morning and Alec's stomach started rumbling. He didn't complain about it, and she refrained from teasing him, finding the whole thing somewhat adorable. Which was strange because she had never been the type to gush over things like "precious" babies or little critters. She dismissed it as temporary insanity. Desert fever, maybe.

They found a nice flat-topped boulder overlooking the valley below where they stopped to eat the leftover tamales that Consuela had packed for them. Off toward Abalone, she made out two dark circling birds, slow and as graceful as two gigantic vultures could be. Condors, a horned-rim-wearing scholar had told her once. Rare, apparently. Their fearsome looks tended to worry folks. As such, these two would likely be dead soon due to some jackass filling them full of buckshot or crossbow bolts.

She glanced at Alec, who was staring at her with a warm expression.

"Why are you looking at me like that?"

"Just thinking about how pretty you are. How smart, too."

She guffawed. "Don't forget ladylike."

"I do like the ladies, I will admit. But a man can't live on champagne and cream puffs. He needs a nice hearty stew or a hank of beef. Something solid. That's what a good, strong woman is."

"You're comparing me with beef jerky? How flattering."

"Now, that's not what I was saying."

She grinned at him. "Relax, Romeo. I ain't no Juliet, it's true."

"You surely are not. You're better." He winked at her.

Then he looked out over the valley, too. She tried not to notice his strong jaw and the sight of his thick wrist, the flash of a sun-browned forearm sprinkled with freckles and blond hairs and corded with long, lean muscles.

Something stirred in the cockles of her shrunken heart.

Now hold on here.

Hold. On.

She formed a picture in her head of cockles—a waving, tentacled mass of tubes (because she didn't exactly know what cockles were). She directed her sturdy Mexican-crafted boot heels to stomp all over them until they were nothing more than a shiny pulp on the desert floor.

But when she looked at him again, her stomach fluttered.

What in the hell are you thinking, Texie?

If it didn't work out with Amos Spartzenhammer, a decent Christian man who eschewed tobacco, spirits, and cursing on Sundays, then it sure as hell wasn't going to work out with Alec, who embraced all of those things with glee. Sure as shooting, he would run off with the first skirt to wink in his direction. And there she'd be with a big belly full of some rambunctious turd just like his father. No, thank you.

It was settled, then. The first chance she got, she'd run him clean out of town and never look back.

Alec gave a satisfied burp and stood up. He fished out a silver flask from his pocket, took a swig, and offered her some of what a sniff told her was whiskey. She declined with a shake of her head.

"After you." He gave a regal sweep of his arm. A grin caused his eyes to crinkle at the corners.

The cockles twitched, trying to come back to life.

Awhile later, she paused at an uprooted agave. Its trunk was as big around as that of a good-sized oak. A single shoot had sprouted from the top and extended up a good twenty feet into the air. Before the whole affair had toppled over, that is. The dead mound before them was a mass of brown, dried out leaves and twisted husks. She studied it, then glanced around for tracks. None, like usual.

Alec studied her expression. "What do you see? More than a rotted old cactus, I suspect."

"This didn't die of old age. It had help. Apaches. They do all kinds of stuff with agaves—make blankets, sandals, eat the heart roasted over a slow fire."

"Apaches. They're the peaceable kind of Indians, right?"

She gave a high, short laugh. "Not usually. The other tribes hereabouts, the Zuni and Comanches, don't much cotton to them. You know why? Because they never took to farming. They took to raiding the other tribes. And Lord, are they fearsome. The Guadalupes were their last stronghold. The cavalry chased them in there a few years back, hoping they would expire since there's nothing much to live off of. They didn't."

Alec paled and gulped. She slapped his shoulder. "Don't worry. They're nowhere around here." She reconsidered. "Probably."

"You sure know how to reassure a fellow."

"It's not too late for you to head on back to town."

He looked her in the eye. His own never failed to surprise her. Sky blue, light like the full sun at noontime. "I'm staying."

"Suit yourself."

Chapter 10

They were scrambling up the side of a dry arroyo, trying to climb up it when from behind them, she heard the cock of a rifle. Alarm seized her gut. She catapulted herself over the edge and grabbed Alec's wrist to haul him up after her. He practically flew over the side and tumbled onto the rock-strewn embankment.

"What the—"

A bullet zipped past with a whine. A *ka-chunk* told her that it hit the trunk of a pinyon pine about three feet ahead of them.

"Meep!" Alec exclaimed.

The two of them shoved each other behind the pine, which afforded the only cover nearby. They scanned the surrounding desert. Everything fell quiet except for the intermittent *ke-ke* of a harrier flying low over the brush to the east. Nothing. Almost as if they'd dreamed the whole thing.

Then Texie saw the glint of metal off a rifle barrel.

"There!"

She pointed east, just beside a crisscrossed collapse of lightning-blackened trees.

"How many?"

She glimpsed a black hat next to where the rifle rested. "Two, at least."

"Make that three." Alec pointed. "Over there, behind the fall of boulders to the right."

"Got him."

She took out Miss Jennie and cocked her slowly to muffle the sound. Alec didn't follow suit. She glanced at him and he shrugged.

"My smooth talking usually keeps me out of most messes."

"Splendiferous." She nodded at the fold between two low ridges. "Let's slide on over there without getting shot. See if they follow."

He caught his teeth on his lower lip, looking nervous. But instead of arguing, he nodded.

"Keep low and make sure to avoid boot scuffs on the rocks."

They moved side by side, hunched over so as to minimize their appearance now that they had only brush to conceal them. Her heartbeat raced like a wild mustang and her breath came in shallow bursts. She struggled to calm both, as she had so many times before in dangerous situations.

Alec's shoulder bumped hers. She had to hand it to him. He could move stealthily when he set his mind to it. He had probably learned that while sneaking out of the beds of married women.

They made it to the ridge-fold. A scattering of rocks and brush separated them from their assailants, and with any luck, it would conceal them, too.

She examined the terrain ahead and made out a faint game trail.

"There." She motioned at a curve in the trail. "Now."

He followed close at her back like a shadow. Said back seemed as big and exposed as a wagon side. Shivers crawled up and down it like hairy spiders.

Calm, Texie. Calm and smarts. They'll get both of you out of this.

She stepped onto the shower of rocks at the S in the trail. Her boots dragged as she put her weight on the uneven earth.

Everything happened at once, then. A bullet ricocheted off the rocks at her feet and sent a spray of dust and stones against her legs. Another bullet whistled right past her arm, tugging on her sleeve like an insistent suitor. Alec bumped into her shoulder. They seized one another's arm and lurched forward.

Their legs pumped as they made for a copse of stubby pines a hundred yards distant. It may as well have been a hundred miles distant for as long as it seemed to take them to get there. She slid on the rocky soil behind the pines with a heave of relief. Alec was a step behind her—still standing. A good sign. He gripped his fancy Stetson in his left hand, revealing that neatly cut light brown hair plastered to his skull with sweat.

The distant sound of men's shouts caused them to exchange glances.

"Come on," she ordered.

She led him up the side of the steep scree to the left of them. Her thighs burned as she ran. A false step in a gopher hole made her stumble. Alec caught her around the hips and propelled her up and forward with a well-needed boost.

Stones and dirt slid down the hill after them. Lady Luck smiled their direction, though. They summited a bald-faced rock ledge, then charged up the hill behind it where a clump of thick brush lined the ridge.

There, they threw themselves down. Their breaths tore in and out of their lungs like smoke from a steam engine. As soon as she wasn't in imminent danger of expiring, Texie got up and parted the spindly branches and tough leaves enough to get a view out the other side.

Just as she'd hoped, she could see downhill to where the bandits were making their way after them. Three of them, all right. One had a stovetop black hat and a long-sleeved black shirt. He moved like a fellow in middle age, a bit stiff around the hips and favoring his right leg. The other two were younger. Brothers, maybe, since they seemed to have the same short, slight build. One of them carried a rifle and the other a six shooter. They didn't seem too experienced with guns since they waved them around. One or the other of them was going to shoot himself in the head if he kept that up.

Alec appeared beside her, too close and not as foul-smelling as she had expected, what with the amount of sweating he was doing. He cupped her right elbow with a gentle hand.

"Let me see your arm. You're hit."

"No, I'm not." She shook his hand off and twisted her arm around to prove it. No blood. But a tiny nick had taken out a pinky-nail-sized piece of cloth from her blue cotton shirt, the one with the white stitching on the front pockets that she liked so much.

Alec sighed in relief. When she puckered her brows at him, his cocky grin made a quick appearance.

"Oh, good. I was going to kiss it and make it better, but I don't much like the taste of blood. I would have done it for you, though."

"Thanks . . . ?"

"You're welcome."

"Can we get back to watching the bad men, please?"

They peered through the brush side by side. A movement several hundred yards away drew her eyes to that flash of the leader's black stovetop hat. What was that at his throat? A white collar, it looked like. The fellow popped his head up, hands cupped around his mouth.

"Alec Malone, you weasel, I know you're up there! I saw that dandified hat of yours a mile off."

Texie startled. Alec paled.

"They *know* you?"

"Err . . . sort of?"

The shout came again. "We know you're after your rattlesnake partner, and we've been tracking you all the way from New Orleans. We don't aim to stop now! Show yourself or we'll give you a taste of this medicine." He whipped up his rifle and fired a shot in their general direction.

Then Stovetop Joe ducked back behind a fall of boulders before she could site Miss Jennie on his big, fat, murderous head.

"Damn it!" she hissed. "Too far away."

"We'll just have to wait until he gets closer then."

Buckshot whistled into the leaves above their heads, making them part and quiver. They came from a shotgun. Which those other three didn't have.

She glanced at Alec, wild-eyed. "More shooters?"

"I'm thinking we found the Bully Flamenco gang," he said.

Success didn't taste so sweet. Texie's eyes darted back and forth as she searched the bland surroundings. Two things happened at once, then. A chorus of shots rang out, and Alec yanked her down to the ground then tugged her with him as he kicked the earth to scoot the both of them back from the bushes.

"What?" She yelped.

"Up there." He pointed to the other side of the canyon, the source of the gunfire.

There, a dozen grubby-looking drifter-types crouched with guns drawn. One of them had a pistolero aimed at her and Alec, and the others mostly gawked down at Stovetop Joe and the Murder Twins. A couple of God-awful big black dogs appeared on the ridgeline behind the newcomers.

"Beelzebub! Homer! Go get 'em!" shouted a gnarl-bearded old coot. He pointed down the hill at the three who had been after her and Alec.

The dogs ran hell-bent for leather down the hill. White foam dripped from their slathering maws.

Times like these called for a particular kind of courage. The smart kind.

"Come on!" Texie ordered.

She ran straight across the hillside away from the commotion. Boots jammed down on rocks and sticks—and once, an unfortunate prairie dog—as they fled like jackrabbits. She managed a graceless leap over a clump of cholla at the last instant. Alec ran right through it with a squawk. He'd be feeling that later.

"There!" He jabbed a finger at an opening in the side of the hill. It looked like it had just enough room to hide them.

They flung themselves into the cave without any chance to check for pit vipers, scorpions, or large rodents. Luckily, it seemed to be empty of everything but dirt and pointy rocks. She rubbed her behind, which would likely be covered in bruises tomorrow.

Even from here, a good quarter-mile distant from those shrub bushes they'd hid behind, they could hear the sounds of vicious dogs and the screams that followed. Both she and Alec winced.

"I don't much like being shot at, but being torn apart by hell beasts seems like a pretty horrible fate," Alec commented.

"Save your sympathy for people who deserve it. We found the gang, I reckon. Now, fess up. Who are the ones who shot at us?"

"I ran across them back in Missouri. You talk about those Apaches being fierce. These fellows are mighty fierce themselves."

"More outlaws?" She felt a chill chase down her spine. What if they were here to join up with the Bully Flamenco gang? They already had upwards of forty miscreants among their numbers.

"Not exactly. Worse, in fact."

"Who, then?"

He looked her straight in the eye. "The Methodists."

Chapter 11

Alec would have told Texie all about the Methodists but for the fact that their first priority needed to be escaping stray bullets to the brain bucket. They tramped through the desert for three hours without a sign of anyone following. He squinted at the barren slice of land that supported nothing much except lizards, weeds, and shale. Texie had decided to veer a mile east of their route out, worried about leading the villains to Ernesto and Consuela's front door. Each step had felt like hell, with cactus spines rubbing and piercing and generally making Alec's life miserable.

Finally, though, they crouched in the meager shade of a mesquite tree and examined Alec's injuries. The sharp spines ranged in size from five feet to twenty-five feet.

"They're two inches at most, you bawl baby," Texie informed him.

However long, they hurt like hell. The needles protruded in the dozens from his shins and knees, a few of them making it into his thighs, too. Peeling his custom-tailored gabardine trousers off was an exercise in torture. No matter how slowly or carefully he went, some broke off. His trousers looked like a baby porcupine had shot its tiny quills all over them. His legs didn't look much better.

Texie popped the needles out with relentless precision. She ignored his cries of pain.

"Ow. Ow, ow, OW. Woman, what the hell?" When he wrenched his legs aside, she stopped at last and looked up at him. Her lips were as flat as her steady brown gaze.

Alec scowled. "Are you just naturally mean or do you have to work at it?"

She harrumphed. After a too-long pause, her face softened. "Little bit of both. 'Course, you're also a puling kitten when it comes to pain."

He considered arguing with her, but she did have a point. Getting punched in the face, run over by wagons, kicked in the ribs by mules . . . all these things he had experienced, and they had hurt like the devil. Tumbling down the stairs at the Desert Rose hadn't been too pleasant either. But somehow, they didn't seem quite as awful as the annoyances he'd suffered on this trip. The raw feet and rumbling belly and 8,000 cactus spines.

She held out an olive branch. "I'll tell you what. I know a way you can be distracted while I finish this up. You won't feel a thing."

He squinted at her. "Yeah?"

"Start talking about the Methodists. The big, scary Methodists. Oooooh." She waved her hands around. Almost as if she didn't believe him.

"Oh, they look harmless enough at first. What with their feeding the poor and ministering to the sick and all that folderol. But I assure you, missy, they have a darker side."

"What did you do to them?"

"Nothing! I was the victim of a foul lecher of a partner and the Methodists' own intemperate need for revenge."

"A victim. You?" She brayed out a laugh. "I am 110 percent certain that is not the case."

"Then you would be 110 percent wrong."

"Just get on with the story, will you?"

He did. It took a while. She sat cross-legged next to him and meticulously tortured him while he sweated and blabbed on. When she was done, she sat back and combed the knots out of her long hair with her fingers. He finished his story at last.

She pursed her lips. "So let me get this straight. You sold them a bunch of Bibles for their missionary work. Twenty thousand, did you say? Then you dumped those Bibles in the river."

"That's just unfair! I told you how it was. They wanted the Bibles delivered to them in some God awful dirt settlement in Missouri that was miles from the railway depot, on mud roads to boot! Then it rained and the river swelled up. They had an important deadline—something about hellfire and brimstone—so we had to get over that river that day."

"And *that's* when you dumped them in the river."

"That's when *God* dumped them in the river. He's the one who sent the rain and made the mules stumble and the wagons tip over. See, an act of God."

She ran a finger along her chin, considering. "You think they would be understanding of that, given their predilections. Why, then . . . ?" Shrewd understanding hardened her eyes. "You took their money."

"Of course not! I refunded it."

She waited.

Sweat gathered at his collar. "Mostly."

A dog bayed in the distance.

"Ah, hell." Texie surged to her feet, scooping up her pack,

bandolier, and Ole Hank.

Alec sagged back against the boulder. "Do we have to run again? Can't you just shoot them?"

"I generally try not to shoot people, believe it or not. Especially when I am outnumbered. If you want to sacrifice yourself as a decoy, I understand."

He sat upright and tugged his trousers on. "You're a cruel woman, Texie Cortez."

She grinned. "I would have seen to it that the *Abalone Monthly* ran a special tribute to your bravery."

A few minutes later found them jogging toward town. Which was a good twenty miles off, according to Texie.

"I never ran twenty miles before." He huffed on.

The barking came closer. Texie shot a wild look at him.

Damn.

In the distance, a rectangular-shaped hut pointed toward civilization. They saw it at the same time, and the goal put an extra spring in their steps. Alec wished he'd put his jock strap on as his twig and berries were chafing and flopping around. He'd have to air them out a bit if he and Texie lived out the day.

A shot rang out. The sound of angry curses and unintelligible rants followed.

"After me!" Alec directed her.

He zigzagged through the brush in an escape maneuver he had used more times than he'd like to admit. It had a pretty high success rate except for that time that Lily O'Reilly's mother caught him and attacked him with a rolling pin. Those things hurt righteous enough that afterward, he eschewed the attentions of red-cheeked gospel band tambourine players for a good month or two.

The hut turned out to be a broken-down prairie schooner that some poor wretch had left behind. Torn canvas from the cover flapped in the breeze. The two front wheels lay in pieces nearby so that the wagon bed tipped down into the sandy earth.

"Turn it over!" he shouted.

The two of them upended it to give themselves some protection from the bullets that they were sure to encounter soon enough.

Texie whipped out her gun and slid bullets into the chamber, fingers not even shaking. Lord Almighty, what a woman! He seized Ole Hank and gripped it hand over hand. He'd been a fair ball player in the streets of New York City when he was growing up.

Side by side, they crouched behind the wagon, awaiting the dogs and their keepers.

A curious angry rush zipped through him, his own sort of Viking Berserker rage. "Bring 'em on!"

Texie grinned at him. There was one thing she approved of.

The dogs arrived first. Both of them were black hounds that slobbered all over the place and growled like the devil. When they charged up, Alec put aside Ole Hank to shout and chuck fist-sized rocks in their direction. That halted them. They stood a ways off and took up baying in deep, loud howls.

Three of what he presumed were the gang burst out of the brush, covered in sweat and ragged around the edges from all that running. Texie didn't wait around. She winged the one with a bandana covering his mouth in the left shoulder. He yelled like a pot of boiling oil had been dumped over his head and fell to the ground, rolling around as he clutched his shoulder. The second dude, a young Mexican fellow, goggled and flung himself into the brush. Texie fired after him.

"Zooterkins!" exclaimed the third, a skinny man with a red beard and crazed eyes.

He whipped out his six shooter, then fumbled and dropped it on the ground.

Alec sprang forward, despite the savagely barking dogs. They lunged at him as he swung Ole Hank in a wide arc. They fell back. Alec practically leapt atop the skinny man and knocked him over. Ole Hank struck him under the chin, making his teeth clack.

The two of them rolled around and elbowed one another as both tried to get the fallen gun. The fellow's stink nearly did Alec in—a sour, sharp, oily type of scent that reminded him of the New York back alleys with permanent populations of transients.

Alec elbowed the stinker in the solar plexus and surged to his knees. This gave him enough space to get a firm grip on Ole Hank again. He gave a powerful swing that connected with the fellow's temple. Crack! He fell over like a stone.

All the while, Texie pumped bullets into the brush. The dude in there returned a couple of shots before he stopped altogether.

The dogs both rushed Alec, then. One went for his neck while the other sank his jaws into Alec's shin. He cried out. With Ole Hank still clutched between both hands, he swung his elbows back and forth in an effort to knock the dog at his throat in his square, hard head. The collar of Alec's fancy shirt tore. The dog's hot breath and spittle moistened Alec's cheek. Alec got some solid whacks against the critter's head, and when that didn't seem to get the job done, he levered Ole Hank into the dog's solid chest and thrust back. It fell back a couple of steps, just enough so that Alec had enough room to whack it in the mouth. That did the trick. It ran, yodeling in pain.

In the meantime, the other dog continued to savage his leg. He swung around just in time to see Texie in front of them. She grabbed the base of the leg-dog's tail and jabbed the two fingers of her right hand up its butt. Immediately, it let go of Alec's leg, squealed like an outraged pig, and took off, tail between his legs.

"Are you insane?" he squawked.

"It worked, didn't it?"

She made a face at her fingers and stuck her hand in the dirt to scrub it clean.

"Why didn't you just shoot the damn thing?"

"I like dogs!"

"Even the kind that rip my legs to shreds?"

"You can't really blame them for that. It's what they've been trained to do. Plus, I didn't want to shoot you instead."

He peered back the way the three had come from.

"More are back there. We need to get going."

She helped him up. He could put weight on his mauled leg fine, but the sight of his torn trousers and the feel of blood running down his shin meant that he had some wounds to attend to later. Texie supported his elbow and they took off at a shambling run like partners in a sack race.

A split in the earth about two feet wide showed evidence of a stream that had once passed through. They leapt across it. Alec's leg folded under him on the other side, and if it weren't for Texie, he would have sprawled on the ground. He was about to charm her with one of his flippant—but incredibly witty—comments when they stumbled right into an Indian camp.

Six heads turned to regard them.

A few half-naked kids lay down in the shade of a mesquite tree. Two women kneeled over a mortar and pestle, and a full-grown man crouched next to them. Said man looked angry. He pointed a nocked arrow at them.

Texie and he froze. They both held up their hands in surrender.

"Apaches!" Texie hissed.

Oh, shit.

Everyone looked at each other for a frozen minute.

Alec swallowed. He liked his handsome face and silken locks so much that he didn't much fancy their being scalped off. There was only one brave. Texie and he might be able to take him, but the women looked formidable in their own right.

"You pew pew?" The man asked in clipped tones.

Texie and he exchanged a glance.

The brave relaxed the arrow to free one hand. He pointed his index finger and thumb like a gun and repeated, "Pew pew."

"Ah!" Texie pointed at the gun holstered at her waist. "Gun?"

"We hear. No like." He gestured at the children, two boys and a girl who sat up gawking at them. "You wake."

"I think he's mad that all the shooting woke up the kids," Alec said. Texie gave him a double-take.

The Apache pointed at Alec and shook his head yes.

"See!" Alec crowed. Then he smiled tentatively at him. "We are sorry. We're trying to run away." He pointed at Texie and himself, then made the motion of running away with his index and second fingers. He jabbed at the air behind him. "They are the ones shooting at us. Bad men."

The Apache considered them without expression.

Texie put her hands together into a prayer and nodded off into the brush. "Please, let us go. We don't want any trouble with you."

They took slow steps in that direction.

"Go?" Alec confirmed. He nodded his head and grinned like an idiot.

The Apache grunted and made a dismissive motion.

"I . . . think that's a yes?" Texie said.

Alec's mouth felt dry. He and Texie clutched one another's arm and made their way past the group. All six faces watched without comment as they went.

Once they were out of sight, they took off running, not stopping for a good mile or so. No one followed them, as near as they could tell.

The afternoon shadows were lengthening by the time they finally stopped for the evening.

"Thank God!" Alec exclaimed.

He flung his valise down, toed off his boots, and whipped his pants clean off. Then he set to examining his dog-bitten shin in what remained of the light.

"Let me see." Texie crowded close.

He hoped it looked worse than it was. Texie inspected the dried blood smeared around the wound. She paled, but before he could comment on that, she ordered, "Give me your whiskey."

He handed the flask over, and she wet his discarded pants with it. Carefully, then, she cleaned the blood off. She looked nauseous but continued her ministrations until she uncovered a full set of teeth marks around a three-inch-long tear. The loose flesh was curling up already. The cut wasn't that deep, though, so he didn't think it needed stitches.

She pulled out her knife. "Want me to cut off the dead skin?"

"Err . . . no thanks. I'll do it myself when we get back to town. After I'm solidly drunk."

She wiped her hands with a grimace and observed as he scratched at his thigh. "Left a few stickers in?"

"They're maddening!"

She held up the knife again. "I can scrape them off."

"Uh . . . I don't think so."

She rolled her eyes. "Make no mistake, Alec. You are a rascal. But I am able to restrain myself from murdering you."

He did not know whether that was a comfort or an insult.

She watched him pick at the remaining needles for a little while before turning around to dig through her pack. She produced a spade. Directly, she started digging next to a clump of brush. By the time he had picked the remaining needles out of his flesh, she had dug a hole about an arm's length across and deep.

"Desert coffee," she explained. "Should be enough moisture collected by morning for a few sips."

He finished buckling his pants on again. The temperature dropped substantially at night so he'd likely need the protection. A strip of dried beef landed at his feet.

"Dinner."

He scoped out a good dirt chair for the evening, a spot big enough for the two of them against a large rock. After he cleared most of the sticks and stones away, he applied himself toward gnawing on the meat, a long, slow, mouth-aching process.

She eyed him. "You were telling me about how you stole the Methodists' money when we were interrupted."

"Oh, yes. Well, as I was saying, I gave them all the money

I had on me, then wired the Riverdale Publishing Company. They're the ones who hired me to do the job. They should be the ones to send the refund, I figured. I didn't dump the Bibles on purpose, as you should understand by now. Well, they didn't much like that idea, and then John Henry—he's the Methodist leader, that fellow in the stovetop hat—got a little excitable and I had to light out or get my neck stretched."

"So now they're after you."

"It would appear so."

She didn't seem surprised. "And the rattlesnake partner?"

"Oh, him."

She made a hands-up gesture that said, "Go on."

His shoulders slumped. "Darlin', it's been a long, long, *long* day. I'm tired and torn all to hell, and I just . . . I don't want to talk about him right now. Please."

"It's quite the story, eh?"

"Yes. Though not all that interesting to anyone besides me, to be honest."

She shook her head. "Why is it that whenever you are within fifty yards of me, there's some sort of trouble?"

"I hate to point out the obvious, but you're a peace officer. Trouble is your business."

"Which makes you my business, I reckon." She considered him. "I was just starting to sort of, kind of, maybe like you a smidgen."

He smiled at her in the gloaming. "I am a pretty likeable fellow, I agree."

"*Was*, in the past tense, Mister. As in, no more."

"You just keep telling yourself that, sweetheart." He patted the space beside him. "Come on over. Let's have dinner and watch the sunset."

"Aren't you romantical."

"There's not much else to do. Unless . . . ?" He lifted his eyebrows suggestively.

She made an exasperated noise but sat next to him. Their shoulders brushed together. A hush fell across the desert. They watched the sun sink below the horizon, all fiery orange and deep pink, the clouds puffed up and soft-looking like squares on a quilt. A coyote warbled about his sorrows, then stopped abruptly.

He noticed her long legs outstretched beside him, ankles crossed. About a tablespoon of whiskey remained in his flask. He handed it to her, and she drained it without a word. Lips on the spout, long line of her throat. He looked away so as not to have her catch him.

"The sunsets were never like this out East. Not once." He wasn't sure he could go back there and stay ever again after seeing such things.

They sat in companionable silence until the colors blazed away into gray. He took her hand. She didn't struggle but merely looked at him with her brows drawn together. Grumpy and recalcitrant. Still fine-looking, though.

He ran his fingers from her wrist up toward the elbow crease, then back down again. Soft, feminine skin. She'd probably be mad if he pointed that out. He smoothed his thumb across the blue vein there. Bending his head, he pressed his lips to the fleshy mound of her palm, then again to the center of her hand. That brought his handsome face a bit too close to her long fingernails, but she didn't claw him to ribbons like a she-cat. He glanced up at her. She was watching him, breath held. The look on her face was . . . indecipherable.

If she were any other beautiful woman, he wouldn't have

stopped. But she wasn't just any other beautiful woman.

Also, she had a gun.

Regretfully, he let go of her hand. Instead, he stretched his arm out around her shoulders. She stiffened but allowed the contact. Slowly, she even relaxed.

"Good night, honey pie."

Just enough light remained to see the grin quirk the corner of her lips. "Good night, cow pie."

He couldn't help it. He laughed.

Chapter 12

At midmorning the next day, Texie and Alec staggered into town. Jimmy Fleetwood and his fellow urchins were throwing dirt clods at each other when they passed by. They stopped in mid-play and gaped.

"We don't look that bad, do we?" Texie glanced down at herself. No dustier and dirtier than usual.

Now Alec . . . the shine had come off his immaculate appearance. His shredded pant legs, limp, and the way he used Ole Hank as a walking stick did make him look ragged and abused.

Rancho McGillicuddy chose that moment to exit the sheriff's office, heading toward the general store. When he glimpsed them, he came running over.

"Dammit all to hell, Texie, what did this yellow-bellied groundhog do to you?"

"Hey!" Alec cried. "I'm completely innocent!"

"For the first time in his life, he's right," Texie said.

In an unusual display of emotion, Rancho kicked one of the dirt clods that littered the street. "You came across them, didn't you? I knew it. I should have been there."

Rancho was like a dog with a bone, hungry and relentless when he was tracking someone down. He would have stayed out in the wilderness to find the gang if it weren't for his granddaughter's violin recital. He hadn't missed one yet, even though it sounded like two cats with their tails tied together. Lord, but he doted on that chubby little girl. Texie supposed she could understand it. Violet was cute as a button.

"Now, you know where you had to be. We survived, although it was touch and go there for a while, I admit."

She went on to tell him about the gunfights and the dogs and the Apaches.

"I have a pretty good idea where the gang has set up camp, so in that way, we succeeded."

"I'll let you clean up and then we'll talk." Rancho scratched the end of his nose. "You should know that there's a situation over at the Crystal Palace . . ."

She already figured that out, on account of Balthazar Gleason running down the street toward her. He clutched an empty whiskey bottle. Behind him, the scorched Crystal Palace swarmed with workers who put up a racket sawing and hammering as they replaced the fire damaged boards.

"Thank God you're back, Sheriff!" Gleason bleated. "A terrible thing has occurred! A heinous crime! I am devastated. Completely undone—"

"Hold up there." She put up a palm to keep him from getting too close to her. "What are you on about?"

He thrust out the empty bottle. "This! Someone put these in the place of my snow globes! The display cabinet was spared from the flames, and I did not discover the theft until a day later when I went to gaze upon their beauty, their unparalleled perfection, their transcendent glory! That's when I discovered their absence."

The fat old degenerate looked close to tears.

"I'll leave you to your business." Alec backed away. "I'm sore in need of a proper washing. Not to mention burning every shred of clothing I've been wearing over the last few days."

She watched as Alec limped away, valise in his right hand.

"Missing, you say?"

Gleason bent her ear for the next fifteen minutes until Rancho stepped in and steered him off to the Desert Rose where he could drown his sorrows in a nice glass of whiskey. Texie knew for a fact that Carlene and Gleason had a contentious rivalry, and each one stole customers from the other whenever possible. She wouldn't doubt it if Carlene spat in Gleason's glass.

Texie headed home, a few hundred yards over. Herman the Hound, a skinny brown mutt that had taken a shine to her, sat in a nice little hole next to her kitchen door. He wagged his tail when she came near and bounded up for a sniff and a wiggle. She didn't like people to see her let him in the house, as the grungy thing was probably swarming with fleas, but she wanted some companionship as she heated the water for a bath and peeled off her dirty things.

Huh. That was odd.

She'd never minded being alone before. Even though Alec had dozens—possibly hundreds—of annoying quirks, his presence did seem to make her feel . . . something. Warmth? Amusement? She couldn't give it a name except to identify that, God help her, she liked it.

An hour later, she sat out on the back porch, tired feet propped up, long, just washed hair drying in the breeze, and Herman dozing next to her. It felt so good to just lounge around without any demands on her time. As good as ice cream right out of the bucket.

Right about then, she heard someone beating on her front door and a voice calling, "Sheriff! We need to have a talk."

Mayor Frasier. The rest of the town council likely in tow.

She considered ignoring him, but that's not what her Papa would do. "This job is twenty-four hours a day, seven days a week," he used to say. Turns out he was right.

With a groan, she lifted herself out of the chair and went back to work.

Town meetings were ever only well-attended when some disaster befell the area, like that plague of grasshoppers last year or the shortage of whiskey the year before. Or whenever the Bully Flamenco gang was hereabouts.

Texie called this one in order to get a posse together, but her simple, straightforward explanation of the returned outlaws was met with a flurry of worry and hysteria. Which seemed to be the default reaction of certain citizens. Lordy, she hated this part of her job. The stern-faced town council members sat on straight-backed chairs behind her, arms folded and mouths shut. They could look intimidating from the audience, but she knew how ineffectual most of them were in reality.

"Now, that is not what I said at all, Mrs. Johnson," Texie objected, trying not to sound as annoyed as she felt.

Mrs. Johnson carried on like she'd never heard Texie. "Then they'll come into town and kill our menfolk and ravage us women. Ravage us, Sheriff! You, too! I cannot fathom why you are not more concerned with hunting down these reprobates!"

A hoarse cheer went up from the jam-packed church.

"I never said I wasn't going to chase them off. Just that Rancho and I can't do it alone this time. There's a good forty or fifty of them squirrelled away in the Guadalupe canyons. You all know how rough and rocky that area is."

Murmured assents rose up, and heads nodded. Texie steeled herself and tried to appeal to reason and common sense.

"Here's what I'm thinking. We put together a posse and head out to track these varmints down, once and for all. Now, it will take a few days or so to get enough men together, but once word gets out to the surrounding farms, we'll have plenty of volunteers, I'm sure."

Mrs. Johnson did not look placated. "But Sheriff, why wait? In three days, Lord knows what could happen! As a woman, I am shocked that you are not more concerned. Shocked! These ruffians have been known to deflower many a young beauty in addition to their other heinous crimes."

Texie couldn't help it. She saw red.

"For Christ's sake, Marilyn. We need a few days to put together a posse, supplies, and figure out our moves. I don't think it's too much to ask that we take time to prepare carefully when we're putting our lives at risk, do you?"

Mrs. Johnson's face flushed and her mouth opened and shut like a fish gasping for air. She sat down abruptly and whispered to her bosom friend and fellow pinch-faced old gossip, Mildred Schoepenhauer.

Marty Hannigan jumped up. "Them Bully Flamencos is a menace. The last time they was here, they ran down all of my goats and six of my chickens! I had to barbeque the lot of them right quick—no time for seasonings or marinades or nothing. What a sorry situation it were."

Voices rose in a confused mishmash. The mayor banged his shoe on the table to little effect.

"Quiet!" Texie roared.

That shut them up. Before they could get started again, she said, "Now I told you we'll be taking care of it! That's what you hired me for, isn't it? And I've been doing a spot-on job of it, despite being a woman and having a uterus and tubes and whatnot." This evoked scandalized gasps from the more pious among them. Embarrassed noises and some giggles rose from many of the others. "That's right. I'm a woman and proud of it! But I can't go hunt down fifty armed shitheads by myself. So go on home, now, and talk about which of you will be joining me in the posse."

Wide eyes and shocked expressions met her tirade.

"Git!" She hollered.

They heaved themselves up off the benches then and made their way out the door. She had time to calm down some as a half-dozen townsfolk pelted her with questions and concerns.

Most people had left when she noticed that Rancho McGillicuddy stood at the back of the church reading some poor soul the riot act. Wait. Not some poor soul. Alec. All scrubbed clean and wearing new duds. The only sign of the ordeal they'd been through was a red patch on his freshly shaved cheek.

He smiled when he saw that Texie had noticed him. Something flipped over in her stomach.

Rancho noticed her approach, too. He ended what appeared to be forceful words with, "And don't you forget it!"

"Yes, sir." Alec sounded strangely sincere.

Rancho grunted, and he nodded at her, then left without another word.

"What was that all about?"

Alec shrugged. "Just a little fatherly advice about how he means to string me up to the nearest tree branch if I do anything to cause you the least bit of discomfort, distress, or indigestion."

Yes, that did sound like Rancho.

"He's got it in his head that being around me is about the worst thing you could do. And while I have seen my share of difficulties, some of which were not even self-induced, I cannot deny that I tend to attract such things."

She cocked an eyebrow at him. "That's right generous of you to admit, Mr. Malone."

He gave a little bow and gestured toward the front of the church. "I have to say, watching you handle a crowd is a truly singular event. Especially at the end there where you went off on that poor screeching grandmother."

"Shut up, Alec."

He glanced away, still grinning but trying not to.

"Why are you here? You looking to join the posse?"

The grin left his face. "What I'm looking to do is to keep you from getting yourself killed."

"That's high-minded of you. I think I'll be all right on my own. Have been so far. "

"I thought you'd say something like that. Damn it."

They walked out into the twilight toward her house. Down the street, she heard the donkeys at the Perkins' place braying for their dinner.

"Guess I'll have to join up too, then."

She stopped and eyed him up and down. "What? Why?"

He straightened his collar and looked proud. "I do have an axe to grind against those malcontents. They nearly blew me to kingdom come, too. And it seems like I won't be leaving town until fall now. Better weather for prospecting. So I'm in."

She started walking again, wondering just how to tell him that he wasn't in. While they did seem to make a fairly competent team when faced with impending doom, his lack of firearm experience made him more of a hindrance than a help when faced with a lot of steely-eyed killers.

"Sheriff!" A panicked voice called from down the street.

Gleason. Again.

"Have you made any progress on the theft of my glorious globes?"

"It's been two hours since I got back into town, Gleason. I'll need at least another hour before I wrap up my investigation."

"Oh, good." He deflated with relief, unable to identify sarcasm when it appeared. "It's just that—"

"I'll handle this, darlin,'" Alec said, low, at her ear.

He led Gleason off, a hand on his back, no doubt spewing a bunch of smooth-sounding snake oil into his ear. The men in her life seemed intent on protecting her tonight. She sorta liked it. Always puffing up like a banty rooster got exhausting.

She headed home where she ate a flapjack, drank a cup of red wine, and slept hard for the first time in days.

Chapter 13

Texie chose the Desert Rose for a meeting place since they had a nice long table big enough to fit Texie, Rancho, the mayor, the treasurer, and the county clerk/bailiff/dog catcher. The group of them shuffled over to the saloon at about noon the next day. A few members of the town council still needed some convincing about the posse, and then there was the figuring out of whom to bring along and where to get enough suitable horses and so forth.

Like usual, plenty of drinkers, diners, and card players filled up the other tables. Alec sat at one. A group of onlookers gathered around the table. They oohed, ahhed, and ogled him like he was the prize attraction in a dog and pony show. Well, now. Would that make him the dog or the pony? He could easily fill either role.

He wore that frilly shirt of his with the string tie at his throat, and his smile was white and pretty. He cut and shuffled the deck of cards with a skilled, professional snap, not even looking at them.

Texie tried to ignore him. Once her group spread out the maps and started arguing about what supplies to gather, route to take, and strategy to employ, she succeeded. Until an impressed murmur rose from Alec's admirers. A woman let out a loud, high-pitched laugh. Texie glanced over to see the maid, Mary Ann, who had fought over him with Carlene. Emotion heated her innards like heartburn. Mary Ann stood close behind him, her hand on his shoulder. So familiar. Well, what did Texie expect? Alec was, at heart, a randy goat that would sooner poke a woman than look at her.

But then he glanced her way and murmured something into Mary Ann's ear. Her lower lip jutted out and she flounced off. Alec winked at Texie. Hot blood rushed to her cheeks. She averted her gaze in an attempt to look like less of a moon-eyed prairie chicken.

John Harkins, the designated note taker, had filled out a piece of paper with two columns—one for potential posse members and one for the supplies. The group made good progress filling out those columns. Nay, they made amazing progress for a bunch of people who took yammering on about nothing to unheard of heights—when the saloon doors opened and Liam O'Reilly lurched inside. He stood swaying as he cast his eyes around the room. When he saw Alec, the look on his face turned blacker than the ace of spades.

"Ye devil! I knew ye had to show your evil face around again sooner or later!"

Liam staggered toward the table with surprising speed. The next thing she knew, Alec was on his feet, hands held out to placate him. The crowd scattered, revealing the garden spade Liam held like a knife.

"Ye stole me job, ye thieving mangy cur!"

Liam swayed. Texie's chair legs skidded across the floor as she lunged to her feet and into the disturbance.

She could smell the liquor on him from twelve feet away. Drunks. They made up eighty percent of her peacemaking efforts. Maybe more.

"Now think twice about this, Irish. You don't want to get brained by that feisty sheriff of ours," Alec said.

"Yer about to lose yours!" Liam jabbed at Alec, who twisted and darted this way and that. Drinks, cards, and coins spilled onto the floor as they jostled the table. Mallard, the resident drunk, skittered over to pluck them up.

Texie jumped in front of Alec. "Hold on! I can't let you stab this card sharp. Though I sympathize with the desire to do so."

"What?" Alec sounded affronted.

Liam pulled back. "Aww, get out of the way, Missy. I can't stab a lady."

"I know, Liam. Let's go have a chat in the jailhouse, shall we?"

She plucked the spade out of his hand and took him by the arm before he had a chance to protest further. She glanced over at Alec. His hat had been knocked off his immaculately groomed head, and he clutched his arm.

"Did he get you?"

Alec displayed a muddy streak down the forearm of his gray coat. "He wiped his grubby paws on it."

She rolled her eyes. "I think you'll survive. Come along, Liam."

Liam must have weighed 200 pounds, all of it solid muscle. She put her arm around his waist to steady him. They weaved around for a good fifteen minutes, stepping in mud puddles and running into support posts along the boardwalk, before they finally made it to the jailhouse.

Liam spewed his tale of woe this entire way, how Gleason blamed him for both the blaze and the theft of the snow globes.

"He fired me, Texie! He fired me from my most excellent job

ever. "Tweren't even my fault." He swung around and jabbed his finger back toward the Desert Rose. "'Twere that slippery snake Malone's fault." Blubbered curses and sobs followed.

Texie recalled her conversation with Alec on the night of the fire. He'd claimed he was in search of an innocent drink. Hadn't he?

"What do you mean? He wasn't supposed to be in there?"

O'Neil paused in the street a few dozen yards from the jail. He sucked up his tears and smoothed down his hair, then spent a moment in composing himself.

"He wasn't supposed to be there, Miss Texie. We had closed up an hour earlier." He tried to enunciate with careful precision. Impressive, considering his lingering inebriation.

"So, you'd closed up already."

"Except fer the reg-u-lars in the back room." The regulars passed out in the back room, he meant.

"And the whores."

"Ah, I see." She tried to curb the disappointment in her chest. "That explains what he was doing there, I reckon."

"No! I take the money for them. I know who comes and goes, I do. It's my business to watch over them."

They came to the sheriff's office. He entered without protest, even when she took him straight into the jail cell and shut the door on him. He clung to the bars and stared at her mournfully, his eyes deep, watery pools.

"No offense now, Liam, but you are drunker than a skunk. You might not be remembering that too well."

"Oh, I remember fine!" He tapped his forehead. "Me memory is stronger than a steel trap locked up inside another steel trap."

She considered him. If she hadn't known him like she did, she would have dismissed that comment as the ramblings of a drunkard. But Liam had a scholarly side, despite his rough and tumble work. More than once, the two of them had sat down at the bench outside the Crystal Palace and talked about the latest news, the works of Walt Whitman and Ralph Waldo Emerson, and Thucydides' history of the Peloponnese. Liam could recite lines verbatim. He could probably even compose something impressive if he gave it a try. She admired that about him.

"I believe you, Liam."

He reached through the bars with a meaty hand. She grasped it and found her hand enveloped by his moist fingers.

"Yer a good lass, Sheriff. Don't let no one tell ye otherwise."

"Thank you, Liam. You're still going to spend the night in here, though."

"Aye . . ."

He let go and lurched over to the cot, which sagged and squeaked under his weight. Within minutes, he was snoring like a steam engine.

She watched him. He wasn't a bad-looking fellow. She might even have favored him if it weren't for the fact that he had at least one wife back home in Dublin. Talk around town speculated that he had another one next door in Kansas.

She spent the afternoon shuffling papers at her desk to the accompaniment of Liam's snores. No matter how she tried to keep him away, Alec stayed on her mind. His cheeky smile. His white-blue eyes. That particular way he ambled along, like he was strolling beside a lazy river instead of going to the outhouse or the saloon. Finally, she gave up trying to work and just sat there sipping coffee and thinking all the thoughts that clamored for her attention.

Liam woke up and groaned pitiably. He squeezed his eyes

shut as though the dying sunlight through the window caused him physical pain. She fetched him a tall glass of water. His Adam's apple bobbed as he downed it.

When he finished, he looked around him. His shoulders slumped. "So I murdered that card sharp like I meant to?"

"Not quite. He's a trial sometimes, I admit. But overall, he means well."

Liam looked her in the eye. His own were bloodshot. "I wouldn't count on that."

The certainty in his voice piqued her attention. "He did drag you out of there before the flames consumed you."

Liam squeezed his eyes shut and massaged his temples with thick fingers. With a moan, he lay back on the cot. "A cruelty, it seems."

He turned on his side and relaxed into sleep again.

Alec was in Higgin's Barn and Grill, raking fresh hay over the stall that served as his room. A blanket and pillow lay atop a few hay bales and his valise and hat sat in the corner. His vest hung neatly over the side boards. His white shirt sleeves were rolled up at the forearms, and the buttons were undone to reveal a few wiry hairs on his chest. She stood and admired him for a breath before he noticed her. His face transformed.

"Hello, my sweet. What a surprise! Come in, please." He gestured at his stall with a flourish.

She looked around. "I thought for sure you'd get your room back at the Desert Rose rather than squat out here like a mule."

He scratched the back of his head. "Yes, well, it seemed safer here than back at the Desert Rose in range of Mrs. Gibson and various pointed kitchen utensils. Plus, Mr. Higgins offered me a few bits a week to watch over the place at night."

She smiled at him, then sat down on the hay bales that served as his bed. His eyebrows rose. She patted the bale next to her.

"Let's have a . . . talk."

She didn't know how to flirt much, had never really had an occasion to do so, but she had seen plenty of sweet young things bat their eyelashes at cowboys. If they could do it, then she could, too.

He looked uncertain but sat readily enough. Then he smirked with one side of his mouth and twinkled his eyes. "What is this, sugar plum? Are you looking to seduce me?"

"You found me out. Come on. There's no time to waste." She leaned back on her elbows, making sure to push her breasts out.

His eyes widened and he gulped. "Are you . . . what is this all about?"

"You'll see." She pitched her voice low and sultry.

He leaned in close. The warmth of his body radiated like hot coals. He smelled like fancy toilet water and cigars. The bastard sure knew how to be even more attractive than he already was . . . and that was saying something. When he moved in for a kiss, she scissored her legs and twisted her hips. They tumbled off the bales, her on top. Alec gave a *whoof* as they landed hard.

"Aren't you a rough one?"

She whipped the handcuffs out of her vest pocket. With a click, she snapped them around one wrist. He grabbed at her hand and she elbowed him hard in the nose. He let out a surprised yelp but managed to snatch at her single long pigtail. They rolled around the floor, grunting and sweating, before she twisted free and pinned his cuffed wrist down with her knee. By leveraging her body weight on his other arm, she snapped the cuff around that wrist as well.

She sat back. He stopped struggling and gaped at her. Straw clung to his collar and stuck in the crease of his perfect ear.

"Are you crazy? What is this?"

She caught her breath. "Alec Malone, you are under arrest for the theft of three European snow globes."

Chapter 14

"So's then she told me, 'Now Flibber, what would I want to go and marry you for if you won't even buys me a ceramic Chinese ceegar box to put my ceegars in when I ain't smokin' em?" He made a hacking snort. "She was a powerful good smoker, my girl surely was."

Alec knew that Texie was a tough woman. Moral and fair. But this? This was beyond the pale. Downright torture. Alec groaned and let his head bang against the bars in his cell. It made a faint twanging noise that Flibber McGee ignored completely. He sat in Texie's banker's chair—the kind with springs—with his mud-caked boots up on her desk, and jawed on. Without ceasing.

Ever.

"Can you 'magine that, mister? I never did hear of anything so peculiar. Not in all my born days. Them Chinese has some powerful good paintings with them little peoples running about and stabbing folks with swords and whatnot. But that don't mean you need one in yer house . . ."

Alec tried to ignore him and go back to sleep, but Flibber wasn't having any of that. He stood at the bars and nattered on so persistently that after a few hours, Alec had no choice but to resign himself to his fate. Some previous occupant of the cell had left a half-carved stick of wood under the cot, so he took to gouging pieces out of it with his blunt, square, unusually strong fingernails, imagining taking chunks out of Flibber's head as he did so.

By the time Texie strode through the front door, he had mostly learned to ignore Flibber, a condition helped greatly by stuffing his handkerchief in one ear and the end of the pillowcase in the other. Flibber never did notice that he wasn't listening.

Alec sat up and unstuffed his ears, his heart warming in his chest. Texie was scowling, like usual. But since she didn't even glance his way, it couldn't have been his fault this time.

"Damn it, Flibber, get your filthy boots offa my desk."

Flibber jumped up as well as he could with the chair squeaking and pitching this way and that. "S–s–sorry, Miz—I mean, Sheriff—Cortez. I'll clean it up."

Texie fussed over the chunks of mud on her paperwork and cussed Flibber up one side and down the other while he scooted the crumbs and clods around to make an even bigger mess.

"All right!" She snapped. "That's enough. I'll take care of it. You go on, now. But come back at two pm."

"Yes, ma'am. I'm eager to make it up to you, I am."

She grunted in acknowledgement as he backed his way out of the doorway, hat in hand. A smack and an "Ow!" told Alec that he had tripped over the steps. Alec couldn't help but laugh.

His smile faded soon enough when he realized that Texie was ignoring him. The clock ticked on the wall. The floorboards creaked as she got coffee, straightened up her arsenal, and mumbled about that idiot McGee.

He settled back on the cot with his shoulders braced against the wall, watching. How strange, but he felt himself content to just feast his eyes on her for however long she allowed it. What a bewitching sight she was, what with that little tilt of her hips and purse of her lips. The way she squinted at the wanted posters on the wall and fiddled around with them so they were straight and not wrinkled. The cut of her button-down shirt and the clip of her square boot heels, the way her vest couldn't quite conceal those luscious curves.

Ever since he was a little one, he'd loved women, especially with their hair done up in pearls and rings on their fingers and bustles at their behinds. He liked them all soft and yielding and smelling like sin itself.

But Texie couldn't have cared less about feminine things, and he couldn't take his eyes off her. She smelled like fresh air and sagebrush, her cheeks shone with natural rosiness, not paint, and her hair fell in straight silky lengths, not a curl in sight. But he itched to feel it slide through his fingers.

The more he watched her, the more apparent his predicament became. Yes sir, he was in trouble. Not because of his current location in jail, though he knew that would have been a hindrance to anyone else. Rather, it was her steadfast refusal to look him in the eye. It made him feel truly wretched.

Just one remedy for that. He spoke up. "You're a cruel woman, Texie Cortez. A cruel, cruel woman to leave me here with that unrepentant windbag."

Her mouth crooked in a smile but she didn't glance at him. Or respond in any other way.

"The blathering just goes on and on like he can't help himself. Is this what it's like for you, listening to me?"

That did it.

"Pretty much."

He chewed the side of his cheek, trying to figure out how to approach the subject of his incarceration. Figuring out stuff had never been his strong point. Improvising, though? That was second nature.

"Texie. We need to have ourselves a discussion—"

"Haven't you had enough talking for one day?"

"It would seem not."

Texie rubbed oil into her leather bandolier. "You about ready to spill the beans?"

He rose and wrapped his hands around the bars. "Now is as good a time as any."

She didn't move. "I'm warning you. I don't want to hear a load of poppycock. Just a confession. You hear?"

"I hear."

She rummaged around on her desk for a few minutes before approaching the cell. Holding up a notepad and pencil, she leaned against the doorpost that led to the cell. "Go ahead, then. I'm ready."

"Do you have to take notes?"

"Oh, I don't want to miss this for anything."

He sighed. "Texie."

She stared stubbornly at the paper. "What?"

"Look at me."

"Why should I?"

"Because I want you to. I want . . . I have to explain to you."

"Don't you mean lie and deny?"

"Er . . . maybe just a tadpole's worth."

She glared at him, dark eyes flashing. "Dammit, Malone, you are the most aggravating bamboozler this side of the Mississippi!"

"That's not all I am. I'm an avenger of the weak, a champion of the downtrodden, a—"

"Filcher of snow globes?"

That gave him pause. "You're all wrong about that. The snow globes probably got burned up in the fire." Then he remembered the empty whiskey bottles he'd put in their places. "Or some desperate cowpoke snatched them. Whatever happened, there's no proof that I had anything to do with their disappearance."

Her eyes went cold and dark, the light that normally shone there sucked away into some cosmic void. "Yet. In the meantime, I have strong suspicion, and it's more than enough to keep you right here. For now."

"Suspicion! Come on now, Texie. I have been nothing but honorable since the moment we met."

She gave a short shrill bark of laughter. "An honorable man doesn't just happen to wander around the desert with his valise."

"I told you—"

"See, here's what I think. I think that you were out burying your booty in some snake pit in the middle of nowhere until things calmed down a bit. Then you could skedaddle out there and retrieve your ill-gotten gains. But you caught sight of me, and being the horny goat you are, figured you'd better follow me."

"Now that's unflattering, if not downright cruel. It also lacks something necessary to hold me here. Evidence."

"Oh, I'll have that a little later today," she said with deadly certainty.

"Do tell."

She stepped close to the bars until they were an arm's length apart. "You see, there's this fellow by the name of Synjun the

Injun. Lives about twelve miles out of town, and Rancho left this morning to fetch him. Pay him six dollars, and he'll track anybody doing anything. Haven't known him to be foiled once. He's the one who's going after your tracks. You know, from that day we *accidentally* met out in the desert? I bet I know what he'll find buried out yonder somewhere. Some heavenly spheres."

He could feel the blood drain from his face.

"I don't know what you're talking about." It sounded weak, even to him.

She leaned in. Where before she had been reluctant to look him in the eye, now she fixed him with a sharp, furious gaze.

"How can you stand there and lie to my face like that? Don't you have any common decency?"

His voice rose. "Oh, no. I have absolutely no decency at all. Which is why you were never safe with me for the entire time we were in the desert together. Even at night, when I could have done whatever I wanted to you."

She sneered. "You could have tried."

"But I didn't, now did I?"

"That doesn't matter. What matters is that you are a lowdown, dirty, despicable thief, and a liar."

The way she spat the words out made his blood boil.

"Why shouldn't I lie and steal? The truth never got me anywhere. Oh, I learned that young, I did. Honest work." He snorted. "Nothing but fool's work. Leastways, that was true whenever I've tried it."

A slight pause. "I didn't know you had."

"Other than that debacle with the Bibles, you mean." He looked aside, feeling sweat gather on his upper lip. He licked it. "Of course I have, but . . . I don't want to talk about it.

It's stupid. I was stupid to ever think I could be an honest, respectable man like everyone wanted me to be. Like you want me to be."

"Being good and steady is not stupid. Neither is being honest."

He gave a bitter laugh. "Oh, it is when you have an unconventional idea, and when you put yourself out there on a limb and hope and try and then—then you know what happens?" He didn't wait for her to answer. "The limb breaks, and there you are, falling through the air, seconds away from a nasty meeting with the hard, cold ground. Then all you have is broken bones, a broken head, broken—"

She stood nearer than she should have, if she had any sense. The top of her head came to his chin. He could have just reached through the bars and pulled her to him, kissed her solid and fierce. Shut her up good.

Instead, he slumped, shoulder wedged between two bars, the rancor drained out of him.

She didn't move back or say anything.

"It was back in New York when I was nineteen. Me and this fellow I knew from the time we were kids opened up a fine little shop on Fourth Street within view of Washington Square. We sold gentlemen's attire." He ran a thumb down the placket of his shirt to skim over the pearl buttons. "I'm good at picking out styles and whatnot, I think you'll agree."

She gave a slight nod.

"We sent all over the place for the best fabric, found excellent tailors, and went to work selling finished goods. I sweet talked the customers and oversaw the tailors and my friend took care of the money and ordering the fabric. We did good. Quite good for a couple of beginners to the merchant trade. I saw all the greenbacks we were bringing in, and it was plenty enough to pay back the loan we took out from my grandpap and put enough away to expand the store and buy myself a house. Or I thought we did, anyhow. One day, the landlord came a calling and I found out that my friend was six months late on the rent. It was a mistake, I figured. Couldn't ask him because he was off on a buying trip in Boston. Went to the bank to get the funds, and lo and behold, there was $1.31 in the account. And my friend, he hadn't gone to Boston after all. Near as I can figure, he took off down south with every penny. So that's what I think of honest work. It gets you nothin' in the end."

She didn't shoot off some sharp retort or tell him how wrong he was. Not like usual. She just stayed where she was, close by. That twist of her lips was gone, too. He could see her chest rise and fall like she was holding something in. Some righteous anger. Some sort of holy fire.

She pressed her body against the bars. With one hand knotted in his collar, she pulled him in and kissed him. Her lips were fierce and hot, like a wildfire whipped up by the wind and blazing through dry grass.

He went rigid with surprise. Then he responded in kind. Lips sought each other and tongues twined together. Their bodies melted into one another, despite the bars that intervened. They clasped one another tight, hands searching and sliding—

She tore away. Blindly, she stepped back until the wall stopped her. Her eyes were wild.

He recognized the emotion he saw there. Fear.

"Texie." His voice cracked. His lips stung from the violence of their embrace.

She raised a hand halfway to her own lips, then turned

around and dashed out the door. It slammed shut behind her. He lunged to the window to see her hurry off down the street like the devil was chasing her.

The jail's front door opened about a half hour later. Alec smiled.

"Couldn't stay away, could you?"

Carlene appeared in the doorway.

"That's rather presumptive of you, Mr. Malone." She raised an artfully plucked eyebrow.

"Carlene!" He cried. "I mean, Mrs. Gibson. I wasn't expecting you."

"Evidently not."

She perused his jail cell with an air of disgust. "So this is where the dissolute of our fine town end up. I must say, Mr. Malone, I didn't take you for a common criminal."

"No, ma'am. I'm as uncommon as they get."

"So I see. It's all over town that you stole Gleason's snow globes. He was overcome with the vapors when he heard about it. He had quite the liking for you. Now I wouldn't be surprised if he storms the jail with a lynch mob."

He wrapped his hands around the bars. "Come here to warn me?"

"Not exactly. He's mostly bluster, Gleason is. Plus, everyone of any skill or lethal tendencies has already committed to the sheriff's posse. No, I'm here because I have reconsidered my earlier animosity toward you. Especially since you are causing Gleason, my competition, so much trouble."

"When it comes to causing trouble, I am happy to oblige."

"Yes. That is abundantly clear. I decided that I had best see you now, before you get yourself killed. You recall the password I gave you for Snarly Pete, I assume."

"Yes, ma'am. Orange lollipop."

"Yes, I did tell you that." She pushed at the cuticles of her beautifully manicured fingers. "But I have reconsidered. That particular password would have gotten you stabbed multiple times."

He felt the blood drain from his face for the second time today.

"Err . . . I'm most grateful for that reconsideration."

She ran a finger along his knuckles. "You don't deserve that fate. Not when I've had a look at the books and it seems that your presence at the card tables has brought in twenty percent more business since you set up shop with me. I would say that is significant. And it would be bad business to get you killed from here to Sunday."

He cleared his throat. She stared him in the eye. This here was a cold woman. He hadn't realized just how cold until now.

"I'm . . . much obliged to you."

She smirked. "Yes, you are. I'd keep that in mind, if I were you."

He nodded mutely.

"Good boy. The correct password is 'pink puppies.'"

Alec stared at her, not sure what to think. He had trusted her before, despite her dubious profession, but now . . . now he understood that the glint in her eyes had one overriding cause. Greed.

"Thank you, ma'am. I'll be sure to pass along your good wishes."

"Oh, no need for that. You can tell Snarly that I'm missing his trouser trout, however."

With a wink over her shoulder, she left. A whiff of expensive perfume followed her. He remembered when he first saw her, how irresistible and intoxicating she had seemed. Now, she seemed wicked and cheap, at least up against Texie.

Texie.

There she was again, filling up his head.

Flibber showed up presently and started blabbering again. Alec stuck his improvised ear plugs back in and tried to distract himself from dwelling on Texie by planning how to get himself to Snarly Pete before the posse blew him to smithereens. The posse wouldn't be ready to go for a few days, at least, he figured. That gave him time to get out of jail and snag a horse and dash around the desert looking for the gang. He was bound to find them since his little sojourn there with Texie provided him with a working knowledge of the area. This time, he'd bring better supplies and a bigger knife.

Yes, he had plenty of time to do what he'd come here for to begin with. Because falling for a bewitching sheriff and her delicious lips had not been in the plan.

He tried to sleep, but his head buzzed and his right leg twitched like it did when he got overtired. Flibber's snores were almost as loud as his ceaseless yammer.

Sometime, long about four am if the stillness of the night was any guide, he jerked awake from a dream. A nightmarish memory, really, sitting tortured by boredom in church with his unsmiling father and squirming siblings. The preacher's eyes blazed with a righteous fire, red and bright. He stared down into Alec's soul as he boomed out, "Vengeance is mine, saith the Lord. Vengeance is mine. Don't you forget that, Alec Malone."

The restless night stretched out, but he must have slept a bit because Flibber's whining from the outer room woke him at first light.

"Aww, damn it all, Mr. McGillicuddy, I don't want to stay here and miss out."

McGillicuddy replied too quietly for Alec to understand his words, but he got the gist of his tone. *Do your job, son.* The floorboards creaked as he exited the door.

Horses neighed and clomped past Alec's window. The murmurs of a few dozen men accompanied the noise. Alec knuckled the sleep out of his eyes. He was never one to lie about in bed when more exciting things were happening. He made it to the window in time to catch the sight of the horses' rumps as they passed by. And there, up in front, rode Texie.

No! The posse was leaving today. Right now.

Which means that he had hours instead of days to get his ass out there and do what he'd come to Abalone to do in the first place.

He looked around the cell and chewed his lip. Flibber stood up and craned his neck to look at Alec. "I'm off to see a man about a horse. You behave when I'm gone."

When Flibber closed the door behind him, Alec said, "Oh, you can be sure I won't."

By the time Flibber sauntered back through the front door, the sun had peeked over the horizon and sweat was dripping off the end of Alec's nose. Good God, what had the man been doing in the outhouse? Composing a symphony? When he saw Alec, he stopped in his tracks and goggled.

"Help . . ." Alec warbled.

"Lands sakes, Malone! What're you doing?"

"Trying to get through the bars. Got stuck." He mewled in pain to emphasize the urgency of his predicament.

Flibber hurried over to the cell. He shoved at Alec's left arm and shoulder, trying to dislodge them from between the bars where they had become wedged in a spectacularly uncomfortable and intractable way.

Alec didn't budge. Flibber hurried into the other room where he flung things around and reappeared holding a crowbar. He jammed it into Alec's chest—marring his favorite nipple, most unfortunately—and wrenched it this way and that to try to free him. Strategic shifting of Alec's body weight worsened the situation.

"Strangling . . ." Alec croaked.

Flibber didn't stop to think how Alec could talk if he was truly strangling. Instead, he ran back in the office to grab the key to the cell. He jammed the key in the lock and dashed open the door. With a spring and a shout, he seized Alec by his free arm and yanked him free of the bars. Alec howled. His shoulder felt like hell and mashed potatoes.

But he ignored the fact that pain momentarily blinded him, and while Flibber was still inside the cell, Alec leapt out the cell door. He flung it shut with a tremendous clang. Flibber had—unwisely—left the key in the lock. Alec snatched it out. He backed away, breathing hard and clutching the key in a clammy hand. His shoulder screamed.

Flibber's mouth fell open. "What're you doin'?"

"Sorry, Flibber. It's important or I wouldn't do it."

Then he rushed out the front door to the street beyond. He'd made it a few dozen feet before Flibber started hollering his name. Alec figured he had—at most—a half hour before someone let Flibber out. Luckily, the other townspeople were mostly absent from the street around the jail, distracted by following the posse parade.

He ducked off the main street and dashed through the back paths before skidding to a stop on the stable's hay-scattered dirt floor. Luckily, old Albert Higgins, the owner, was absent. Alec had been scoping out the permanent inside residents for some time now and had settled on his perfect getaway horse, Maisy May, a gentle, not too tall blonde filly. Pudgy little Violet rode her when she got around to it, which was pretty seldom.

Maisy May's stall stood empty. So did his second choice, Blackie, a shiny black gelding with a white star on his forehead.

"Shit!"

He didn't count on the fact that the posse probably took all the best mounts for themselves. They left a few behind, though. A yearling that had never been saddled, a couple of too-small-for-riding donkeys, and a lumpy-headed cross-eyed mule named Ralph.

Ralph it was.

Alec scooped up his valise where it lay hidden next to the saddles. Then he fiddled around positioning Ralph's halter and reins for far too long before he twined his fingers in Ralph's wiry mane and swung onto his back without a saddle, blanket, or thank you very much.

"Giddyap!"

Alec hung on for dear life as Ralph trotted out the door and headed west to parallel the posse.

Chapter 15

Texie left the posse at their lunchtime rest spot, some of them dozing under the thin shade of a couple of manzanita trees, and made her way a few hundred yards to the east where Rancho crouched next to an eight-feet-tall stand of cholla cactus. She lay down on her belly next to him, mimicking his posture. Together, they squinted across the salt flats under the afternoon sun. The Guadalupe Mountains sat far and purple at the end of their gaze. In between the two lay dry arroyos, weather-cracked earth, and the inevitable scrub brush, cactus, and rocks. A motion in the bushes about fifty yards away caught Texie's eye. A jackrabbit paused up on his hind legs and looked straight at them. His big, fan-like ears seemed as long as the rest of his scrawny body.

"I'm not so sure this was a good idea," Texie admitted.

They had decided to split the posses up, all the better to cover more ground. Out here, it was easy to miss tracks and paths in the ditches and ridges. Rancho would lead one of them while Texie would lead the other.

Rancho cast a sidelong glance at her. "Don't be doubting yourself now, missy. They won't be expectin' us from this angle and you know it. They won't be expectin' us to split up, neither. Sure, it might take us a bit longer to make our way to the Bullys' camp, but better that than getting laid out by an ambush on the other route."

She turned around and leaned up against the rock she'd been peering over. Caliche littered the ground here with monotonous tan boulders and smaller crumbled rocks, stones, and pebbles. A few straggly weeds struggled to life through that thick, hard soil, but not many. Her Ma had a garden in similar soil at home, so hard that it took Papa two weeks to dig the rows with a pike. When they planted carrots, they grew U-shaped on account of the unloosened ground underneath.

Rancho turned around himself, sitting next to her, knees bent. He rested his elbows on them, took off his hat, and ran his fingers through his short, coarse salt-and-pepper hair. A ring of dust darkened his hairline.

"You ready for my group to head off, then?"

"Think so. No use in waiting."

Rancho nodded, but he didn't move except to put his hat back on his head.

"What about that feller followin' us?"

She'd noticed him, too. "I figure he's a mile back. You?"

"More or less. I found some tracks when I went out for a piss this morning."

She raised an eyebrow at him. "That's some trip for a piss."

He quirked a grin but otherwise didn't reply. He'd never been much of a talker, even back when he'd been her Papa's deputy.

"I'll take care of him," she offered.

He didn't try to talk her out of it. She'd always liked that about him. He respected her despite the fact that she was a woman. The same couldn't be said of a lot of the other men about. It was nothing like back East, though. Women concerned about clean petticoats and combed hair didn't last long out West.

"Could be Injuns. Or the Parsons' kid. He didn't much cotton to being left behind."

She searched the brush. From somewhere out there, she could feel eyes on her. Their pursuer hadn't made a move yet, but that didn't mean he wouldn't. He could just be a scout for the gang. Or . . . well, she could drive herself crazy speculating. There was one way to know for sure.

With a groan, Rancho lifted himself to his feet. She heard his knees pop as he did so. They made their way back to the posse and roused the lot of them.

Texie explained how they were splitting up and made them count off (which two of them needed help with, once they got into the teens). When the most contentious of the lot, Chigger Antoine, opened his mouth to protest, Rancho snapped, "Shaddap. This is how it's gonna be."

For once in his life, Chigger didn't argue.

Rancho motioned at the twelve men who made up his party. They began to gather their gear and saddle up their mounts. With his characteristic limp, he stalked after them.

"Deputy," Texie said.

He stopped and looked back at her.

"You take care of yourself now, you hear me?"

He nodded. "You'd better do the same, missy. I'd sure hate to break in a new sheriff."

He left. She followed him, getting the remaining men—thirteen of them—packed up and on their way. She put a beefy cowhand named Milo in charge. He looked terrified at the responsibility but tried not to show it. She'd rather have someone like that as a leader than a hotheaded fool who couldn't wait to start a gunfight.

Milo waved as the party left at a slow lope headed north. Rancho took his men on a northwestern route. When one or the other of them located the hideout, they'd send messengers to the other posse and approach it from two different directions. If everything worked out as planned. She tried not to think about just how unlikely that was, what with the need to search the endless defiles and rocky promontories, all of which provided nearly unlimited opportunities to hide bad hombres with good aim.

She left her trusty mare, Little Min, with the posse and crept off after their pursuer, senses sharp and belly knotted up and empty. Tracking on a full stomach made her sluggish and lazy. Tracking on horseback made her feel too exposed.

Half an hour later, she had circled around and come up behind the sneaky devil. He was riding a mule, though "riding" might be an exaggeration as she found a butt-shaped impression in the ground and some boot tracks that ran around in circles, showing that he either got bucked off or fell off the mule's back. She studied the fellow's unusual boot impressions. The heels stood taller and the toes narrower than what the cobblers around El Paso or San Antonio put out. The sole was in good condition, too. Practically new. Not worn through and cracked like so many others she'd seen on the miners, dirt farmers, and range riders here about. It was almost as if they were the property of a fancy dude. A dandified gentleman. A . . .

Just past a mesquite tree whose dried-out bean pods littered the ground, she caught sight of a black swishing tail and two gigantic upright ears. The rider had wide shoulders and a hat she recognized. His chin tipped at an infuriatingly familiar angle.

"Dammit all, Alec Malone!" she shouted, unable to contain herself.

He jerked in response to her voice and sawed over to the right. Old Ralph, that broken-down hee-haw, let out an angry snort and wiggled his rump in such a way that Alec's frantic attempts to stay on the mule's back failed entirely. He flew sideways and landed hard on top of a little patch of dried-up weeds with an involuntary cry of pain.

With doleful eyes, he looked up at her. "Every time I see you, I get more banged up than a musket at a turkey shoot."

"Every time I see you, I get more apoplectic than a sixty-year-old hussy with a drunken sot of a husband."

"The longer we are around each other, the more colorful your metaphors are getting."

Alec picked himself up. He winced and clutched his shoulder. The sight of him with a day's growth of beard on his chin, disheveled and dusty from his ride across the desert and his recent acquaintance with the ground, pushed the outrage and surprise away. Something warm and happy took its place, despite herself. Then she remembered flinging herself at him and felt her cheeks catch fire.

She tried to control herself. "Two questions. What'd you do to dumb old Flibber? And why in the hell are you out here after us?"

"Relax. I just locked him up in the jail cell. He's fine. As for what I'm doing out here . . . well, darlin', I was worried about you."

"That's a load of horse crap."

He shrugged and hissed in pain. "I've got a grudge against those bushwhackers, too, you know."

"You don't strike me as the revengeful type of man."

"Maybe there's a lot you don't know about me."

She approached. "What's wrong with your shoulder?"

"Nothing much."

"Let me see."

He unbuttoned his shirt awkwardly with one hand, then pulled the fabric away to reveal his black and blue shoulder. A vertical line went from the top of his shoulder to his armpit.

"It's just a bruise." His voice was low. He was standing awfully close to her.

She jerked back. "I suppose you'll live. And I suppose I don't want to know how you got that."

He forced a smirk. "Probably not."

Ralph nudged her left arm and snorted. "All right, you hog." She dug one of Mrs. O'Malley's sweet green apples out of her pack. He peeled back his huge lips and chomped into the fruit with yellowed teeth.

She put a hand on her cocked hip and looked Alec in the eye.

He squirmed. "What are you going to do with me?"

"I *should* handcuff you to the nearest tree and leave you there until we do what we set out to."

"That would be a terrible mistake."

"You're probably right," she admitted. "I can't fiddle around with you right now, so come on. This doesn't mean you're off the hook, though. Not by a long shot."

"Yes, ma'am. And no, of course not. You can punish me all you like at a later time. I might even enjoy it."

She knotted her fingers in Ralph's mane and swung onto his back. Getting Alec up there required a great deal more huffing, puffing, and flailing about, but eventually, they managed it. She was uncomfortably aware of the feel of his body right up against hers. *His wicked, thieving body*, she reminded herself. His going-to-hell-in-a-handbasket body.

They started off. And despite the fact that he was a thief and a rogue and a tomcat, she found herself leaning back against his chest ever so slightly because it just felt so damn right. The wrongest things did, she knew.

Several hours later, after a half dozen arguments, four double entendres, and some laughter—willing and easy on his part and unwilling and hard on hers—they joined up with Milo and the others. They'd set up camp on the lee of a hill behind a convenient tumble of boulders. Cookie already had a pot of beans going, and the smell made Texie's mouth water and Alec's stomach rumble.

"Don't get too excited about dinner," she warned him. "Cookie's been known to season his beans with shoelaces and dirt."

"At this point, I don't believe either would bother me."

"Let me guess, you neglected to bring much in the way of supplies on your jaunt out of town."

He shrugged, grimaced, and cradled his wounded arm.

Milo caught sight of her. His face transformed with joy and he practically skipped forward to hand command back to her. Their trip thus far, he reported, hadn't consisted of much but evading a herd of javelinas. Also, Roger Cartwright got his right foot stepped on by his horse. Said foot had swelled to the size of Roger's head, and he looked ready to vomit from the pain, but he wouldn't hear of heading back to town. Instead, he lay on his blanket with his foot propped up on a rock, pulling on a whiskey bottle with enthusiasm, his eyelids heavy.

Texie took care of Ralph, telling him what a good strong boy he was and stationing him around a not-too-dried-out patch of weeds with the other mounts. It was all Alec could do to stagger around, bowlegged and sore from the long ride.

She took her canteen and headed off into the brush to clean up.

Alec noticed like he noticed everything.

"Need some help?" he offered cheerily.

Her mouth quirked up in a grin until she remembered that she was supposed to be scowling at him.

By the time night fell, they lounged around the fire with bellies full of beans and bacon. Alec sat opposite her, surrounded by eager listeners as he relayed a preposterous tale about a faro game he'd once played on a riverboat. The participants included a red-haired midget, two kings from Oman, and a circus juggler whose pet was a fifteen-pound rabbit wearing a miniature tuxedo. She shook her head. Alec sure could weave a tale. He had perfect timing and inflection and a talent for making outrageous faces. Watching him, she couldn't help but feel amused.

Then she got to thinking and that amusement faded right away. With a twist in her belly, she got up and picked her way across the dark, rocky earth to check on the horses that were hobbled at the edge of camp. Little Min whickered when Texie approached and mouthed gently when she held out her hand. Min's whiskers scratched a bit, but her questing lips were soft like always.

Texie busied herself with brushing Min, and when she'd done a thorough job of that, she stood there resting her head on Min's shoulder. Papa had given her Min as a filly when Texie was fourteen years old. She couldn't imagine a better horse, or frankly, a better friend. Texie had told her all her secrets over the years, and Min had kept them to herself.

Back at the campfire, laughter erupted. Then someone called out, "Deal 'em quick, Mister Alec!" The crack of expert card shuffling sounded next.

For a while, she leaned back on Min's saddle, which sat on the desert floor, and took in the shadows, night bird calls, and thickened sage scents of the dark. It was still, here, and familiar. A place man and all his hubris could not touch. The immensity of the quiet earth stood everlasting and regal instead. This, here, was why she could never live in one of those huge, smoke-filled cities out east, loud and busy, the rattle of loaded wagons, streetcars with screaming brakes, and the rush and chatter of thousands upon thousands of city folk.

"Texie. What are you doing out here?" A voice came from the dark. Low and sweet.

Alec.

She got to her feet, embarrassed to be caught alone and dreaming.

He approached, a tall, lean shadow. She picked up Min's brush again and set to grooming despite the fact that Min's coat was already smooth and gleaming. But she needed to do something with her hands.

"I'm surprised your adoring fans let you leave them."

He scratched the back of his neck. "Yes, well, we played a couple of rounds and I won cash off most of them. They don't seem so adoring now."

A cold gust of wind swept across the desert. Brush rustled, and the cooking utensils hanging from Cookie's table banged together. She shivered. The temperature during the day was pleasant for the most part, unless you were running around getting shot at, and then it was fairly warm. Night in the desert, though, was way colder than seemed reasonable. All the greenhorns from east of the Mississippi commented on it.

A warm jacket settled around her shoulders. Alec stood behind her and made sure it enveloped her properly. She felt small but protected. He rested his hands on her arms. She wanted to press up against him, to feel his strong arms around her, to smell the scent of his skin. Instead, she shrugged away.

"Hey now, don't go," he complained.

He reached for her and she ordered, "Stop."

He froze. When he spoke, he sounded hurt. "I don't understand. What have I done?"

She snorted in disbelief. "Think hard. I'm sure it will come to you."

"Err . . . the whole jail thing?"

"Yes, Alec, the whole jail thing."

"But—"

"I don't want to hear your excuses or explanations or any of it. I'm a sheriff. I was raised by a sheriff. I can't abide kissing on some criminal, no matter how I . . . it's not right."

"I'm not just some criminal, Texie."

The new moon kept him in darkness, but the dim light of the stars shone around his form in bright pinpricks. Out here, the stars were so thick and alive that their patterns and trails told stories. She thought of all the bad men she'd encountered since she became sheriff, the land grabbers and robbers, the rapists and flat out murderers. They all had their stories, too. Dark stories of evil that twined around their souls like thorny vines. That evil appeared in varying degrees among those bad men, devouring goodness and innocence. Not all the time, true. But enough to separate them from the rest of the folks, to make them look at others like marks, like sources of what they wanted, not friends. And Alec . . . he wasn't anywhere near that bad. He did have a certain charm. A certain barely resistible charm. Still, he had that same basic unwillingness to follow the law.

The smell of him saturated his jacket. Castile soap and tobacco. Toilet water and forbidden lust. With a knot in her throat, she said, "You're a thief, Alec Malone. I can't have anything to do with you. Other than let you fill up my jail."

She could tell by the way he straightened that her words jolted him.

"I can't even be sorry about that," she said with some regret. "Because it's who I am. Who I was born to be. Now you see why you need to leave me alone."

She turned and stalked back to the fire. His eyes bored into her as she went. She didn't need to look over her shoulder to confirm that. She could feel them, like twin fiery arrows.

Chapter 16

Texie's posse proceeded at a restrained pace for the entire morning. She rode in front and spent most of the time peering down at the earth for tracks and at the surrounding brush for signs of their quarry's passing. Fifty or so outlaws running around the mountains would leave some sort of trace, no matter how skillfully they covered it up. But while she could track better than most of her men, she was by no means as good as Rancho or Synjun. The strain of constant vigilance made her eyes sore. By the time they stopped for grub, her head pounded.

That afternoon, they ascended into the foothills. Their pace slowed as the horses picked carefully over the slippery shale and around brush that harbored rattlesnakes. A couple of those snakes shook their tails in protest but didn't strike. Texie dismounted to lead Little Min up and down mound after mound to save her the strain. The rest of the party did the same. At the warmest part of the afternoon, they paused on a rock outcropping that looked down over a canyon. Milo whipped out the spyglass he got from his ex-sailor grandpappy and scanned the terrain. Salt cedars and juniper trees clogged the dip between the two tallest mountains, and the water from the stream had greened and thickened the brush here as well.

All of a sudden, he jerked and let out a yip like a frightened coyote. He thrust the spyglass toward her. "Glory be! I think that's one of them!"

She squeezed one eye shut and jammed the hot brass contraption to her other eye socket. The figure of a man loomed like a twenty-foot giant in her sight. She startled, then handed the glass back to Milo before scrambling to her feet.

"You don't need that, you dimwit."

Milo blushed and got to his feet next to her. She might have felt bad about castigating him except for the fact that a man approached them from barely a hundred yards off. He was leading a pretty palomino whose head hung low in exhaustion. A man who didn't take good care of his horse wasn't much of a man, in her estimation. Though he didn't seem to take good care of himself either. He wore a torn black button-down, dirty jeans, and a square-topped hat. His staggering cadence and dusty appearance told her that he was a tenderfoot.

When he noticed them, he waved. "Howdy, folks!" He moved toward them with coiled enthusiasm, the energy bursting out of him. A youngish fellow—not much past thirty, with bony features and a ridge on his forehead. He had a wolfish cast to his face that suited him somehow. A switch of vague familiarity tripped in her brain. She studied his face but figured, after a moment, that he must remind her of some vagrant or another.

He approached and shook hands all around, grinning like a cat who ate a couple of canaries.

"Boy, am I happy to see you! I've been here, there, and everywhere around these hills, and the closest I've come to humans is a couple of graves out yonder."

"You're lucky you haven't been put in a grave yourself, Mister

. . . ?" Texie asked.

"Hanolon Grant." He gestured at his saddlebags. "I'm a surveyor for a consortium of mining interests, and I've been taking note of this area for three days now without seeing a soul. These mountains show promise for limestone and copper, maybe some silver, too, if I'm not mistaken."

Texie thought about it. "Every now and again, a few miners try their luck out here. Them and the outlaws."

"I could sure use a few coffee beans if you have 'em to spare. It's awful going without coffee . . . wait. Outlaws, you say?" His voice rose in alarm.

Milo snorted. "Lots of 'em, Mr. Grant. The Bully Flamenco gang is hereabouts, and if you don't want to get caught in the crosshairs, you'd best skedaddle. That's why we're here. We aim to bring them rascals to earthly justice or heavenly reckoning, whichever suits the occasion."

Grant twisted his lips and thought hard. "I'd better watch my step, then. I can't be cutting my job short just 'cause of a few malcontents. I promise to be careful as I can, though. Yessiree. Thanks for the warning, fellers—and ma'am. I believe I'll follow it."

They chit-chatted for about ten minutes to be polite and also to find out if Grant had seen tracks or burned out campfires that indicated the gang's presence in the area.

"Wish I had, Miss Sheriff. It would have felt less lonesome if I'd seen evidence that people were about. I didn't even see any Injuns."

"You wouldn't have."

He tipped his hat. "'Spose you're right on that account."

He gathered the filly's reins but dawdled until it became obvious that he was waiting for something. Ah, yes. The coffee.

"Roger, share some of our coffee beans with Mr. Grant, will you?" she directed.

Grant dug a pouch out of his overstuffed saddlebags—no wonder his poor filly was tired out—and held it open to receive a couple of handfuls of Roger's specially roasted stash.

Then he shook Roger's hand, waved to the rest of them, and took off in the direction that the posse had just come from.

As soon as Grant had gone off, Alec dropped Ralph's big misshapen hoof and stood upright, resting his arms on Ralph's swayed back. He'd been picking at the mule's shoes, it looked like. Now that she thought about it, he hadn't said anything but had stayed aside.

He didn't comment, just watched Grant's back as he disappeared into the brush, his mouth a flat line and his shoulders tight. Why, he looked downright unfriendly. She drew her brows together. "You got something to say about Mr. Grant, there?"

Alec gave a "Who, me?" shrug and his face transformed into its usual cocky expression.

A thunderhead built in the south, all white and gray mountains of clouds. The breeze felt a bit humid, too. Rain by the morning, she figured. Papa had said she was gifted in the art of weather prognostication. She was seldom wrong.

"Let's get a move on," she said.

Alec was slow to mount old Ralph. He kept glancing off as though Grant would reappear, guns blazing. He didn't, of course, and soon, she forgot all about Alec's odd reaction.

Chapter 17

By the time Alec could sneak away from the posse, it was around midnight and the sky had started to weep softly. Like the tears Texie would cry when she woke up and found him gone.

He laughed out loud. All the devils from hell would put on parkas before that would happen, not from Texie.

Gallows humor. It was the only way he kept his head about him after the man he'd chased across thousands of miles had just waltzed into camp as easy as could be. Like Alec hadn't spent three long, eventful, occasionally horrible years looking for Mr. Randy Potkalitski, his sticky-fingered ex-partner.

The lies rolled off a tongue as smooth as polished glass. Hanolon Grant, the surveyor. Ha! Surveyor of everyone's valuables, more like.

At first, Alec had been too frozen with surprise to react, but once he shook off the initial shock, he ducked his head behind Ralph to stay out of Randy's sight. As tempting as it was to charge at the thief and wring his neck, it wouldn't get him his money back. Nor would it keep either of them out of Texie's jail, which was undoubtedly where both of them would end up sooner rather than later.

No, this was best.

Follow him and surprise him, confront him alone and lift all that coin from his "supply bags" out of sight of all those yahoos in the posse.

Out of sight of Texie.

Alec had learned a few things watching Texie track, like how to look for broken twigs and scuffed earth, plus, he found a game trail through the brush. The gray glow from the rainclouds lent plenty of light to his efforts.

He walked as quickly as he dared until his legs burned. He'd had to leave Ralph behind for fear of alerting the drowsy guard and waking the others. Not that Ralph would have gone a lot faster than him.

When he passed a boulder, he nearly ran into Randy's palomino tied to a scrub oak, head hanging as she endured the steady rain.

Randy was hunkered down against the boulder. He cursed and leapt to his feet.

Alec couldn't help himself. He lunged at Randy. His fist piledrove straight for Randy's jaw. The blow landed with solid, painful precision. Damn, but the cretin's jaw was *hard*. Randy's head whipped back, and he stumbled to the side, then recovered and rushed Alec. He rammed head first into Alec's midsection and drove him right into the palomino's hindquarters. Alec cried out as his sore shoulder struck the horse. The palomino squealed and kicked. Her sharp hoof caught Randy's hipbone with enough force to twist him 360 degrees around.

Randy had no more ceased spinning than Alec swarmed him, head low and fists swinging in a rapid *bam-bam-bam*. Randy sprawled on the sandy ground, Alec on top of him. He writhed and struggled. His elbow connected with Alec's eye socket, and he grabbed wildly for Alec's shirt, hair, ears, anything he could get his hands on.

Three years' worth of anger boiled to steam in Alec's fists, and he hit Randy again and again on his cheek, nose, and belly. Randy hunched to protect his vital organs, but Alec moved too quickly. The rapid assault sent Randy sliding to the soil. His mouth slackened and his eyes rolled back in his head before he slumped into unconsciousness. He didn't stay out long, though. By the time Alec found his favorite hat atop the boulder and dug a handful of sand out of his boots, he was stirring.

Alec crouched beside him, senses hyperalert. His muscles thrummed from exertion.

"What the holy hell—" Randy slurred. He managed to get to one elbow and rested there as he squinted at Alec. He squinted his eyes and goggled at Alec as though he was trying very hard to figure out who he was. "You look like . . ." he trailed off. "It can't be."

"Au contraire. It can, and I am, Randy."

"You . . . *Spurge?*"

Alec didn't reply. Hearing the old nickname on Randy's lips, delivered in the same familiar tones . . . it stung like an irate hornet.

Randy adjusted his jaw gently and hissed when it popped and clicked. "Always thought you were a talker and not a fighter."

"What's there to talk about? You stole from me and ran off like a coward. The business went broke, and where were you? Gone with the wind. That tells me all I need to know."

Randy's eyes widened. "The business went broke? No, I don't believe it."

"Liar."

"But . . . I left instructions with Mr. Skinner to keep things running along like normal. That old crook kept the money for himself?"

"Like you didn't know."

"I . . ." Randy wiped his mouth and shrugged. "I didn't, Spurge. I cashed out of the business, sure. It was just time for me to go. I'm a rolling stone, you know that, and I was gathering too much moss there in New York. I thought Old Man Skinner would do right by you."

"You damn well did know what you were doing. Admit it!"

Randy sat up with a groan. "You think I would do that to you? Spurge, I've known you since you were knee-high to a toad. I may be a rascal and a devil, but I've never betrayed a friend. Not like that."

Doubt seeped in around the edges of Alec's anger. Randy could lie like a whore in her crib, but what if . . . ?

"If that's so, then why did you just take off without a word? You owed me that, Randy. At the very least."

Randy's eyes flicked to the desert floor. His voice fell. "'Cause I knew you'd talk me out of it. I'd stay and I'd get more and more restless and angrier, and I'd end up hurting you even worse than I would by leaving. I figured it was better for both of us if I just went on my way. That's the God's honest truth."

The God's honest truth.

Randy had said that to Alec a couple of times back when they were growing up together and in the years afterward. Each time, he'd meant it. Alec knew he had. Randy had a few years on him, just enough that Alec had worshipped him like the big brother he'd never had. For a long time, he'd believed that Randy could do no wrong. Lately, he'd been certain that Randy could do no right. And now, he wanted that earlier certainty back.

"I don't believe you, Randy." He tried to put force and certainty behind the words. "And truth be told, I don't care about your reasons. I want what's mine. Sixteen million dollars. That's my share, plus compounded interest and travel fees and a bit of a markup for whatever in the hell I want. Hand it over."

Randy guffawed. "That's preposterous! I maybe owe you $16,000. Maybe. Anyway, I'm carrying about $16.00."

"I know you, Randy. The only time you've been without a load of cash is when you're skinny dipping or soaking in a bathtub, and even then, you might have some jammed up your—"

"Whoa there, cowhand. Let's not be talking 'bout my nether regions."

They sat and looked at one another in the sudden silence. Rain pattered the ground and laid the spindly branches of the sagebrush low with silver-tinted moisture.

Three years had passed, yes. And not all of them filled with woe and heartbreak, if Alec was completely honest about it. When he left New York, he had at first wandered down the East Coast, then made his way west. The Mississippi River and her constant stream of gambling parlors and riverboats captured him for a good year on their own. Then he jumped from town to town, staying in some longer than others but always moving relentlessly west, chasing rumors and sightings of Randy with revenge for fuel. The fact that it was within sight made his head spin better than a bottle of Tejas lightning.

Randy observed him with a cock of his head and an upturned corner of his lips, a familiar expression that Alec had always taken as a sign of affection.

"I don't care that you did just paddle the shit out of me, Spurge. It's damn good to see you again after so long."

Something painful and unwilling twisted in Alec's gut. He ground out, "Don't you say that to me, Randy. Don't you lie again."

"I'm not lying, Spurge. Life on the lam . . . it gives a fellow time to think. A lot of time. Maybe there's a thing or two that I regret. To do with you."

Alec snorted. "Is that an apology?"

Surprise unfolded on Randy's face. "I do believe it is, Spurge. Will wonders never cease?"

A quiver started deep in Alec's belly. It spread to the rest of him. His leg juddered and his shoulders shook. He tried to keep his teeth ground together but the force was too strong. Laughter brayed out of him.

He was having some sort of fit. He'd probably die from it.

In the meantime, he laughed, one arm around his belly. Tears of mirth leaked from his eyes.

"You about done there, Spurge?"

He settled down finally and wiped the tears away. "I s'pose so."

Randy smiled, white teeth under gray clouds. "I'm not sorry I left. New York is cold as a witch's tit in the winter and hot as hell in the summer. I chewed up that place until all the flavor was gone. I could either spit it out or swallow it and choke on what remained. Plus, it smells like shit."

Alec huffed in agreement. It really did smell like shit, what with all the horse manure and garbage in the streets.

"But I'm sorry about Mr. Skinner. I thought he'd do better by you."

Alec rested his elbows on his cross-legged knees and allowed his head to sag into his hands. "He always was an old cheat at heart. Why would you think he would change?"

"Guess I didn't think. That's the problem."

Randy shrugged, loose-limbed. He turned his face upward to the sky and blinked as raindrops fell on him. Alec wiped blood off his knuckles.

"Get up. You're coming with me to the posse."

"Why would I do that?"

"Because I'm telling you to."

Randy searched his face. Alec had no way to force Randy to go. But he had perfected his poker face in the last three years.

"S'pose that's the least I can do for you." He groaned as he got to his feet.

They walked side by side, boots either sinking into the increasingly sandy earth or twisting this way and that on the rock-strewn ground, leading poor Susie the palomino. Dawn lightened the desert sky and the birds came awake.

Randy eventually asked, "Say now, you're not thinking of turning me in, are you?"

Alec cast a sidelong glance at him. "That just occur to you?"

"Actually, yes. Huh. Guess I can't get you your money back, after all."

"Ah, here it is. Your patented line of bullshit."

"You gotta admit, my schemes do work out, occasionally."

Alec didn't want to admit it, but he was right. He tried not to let it show. "What, with your 'surveying' activities?"

"Not exactly. I'm after the Bully Flamenco gang. Got myself a mind to take a share of the loot they have stashed with them. We can split it. Then, if you want, we'll turn them in to that lady sheriff back yonder. Get their reward and split that, too."

"I'm fairly certain it won't go that easily."

"Aw, you know me, Spurge. I'm all about easy. And I've been planning this out for a while now. You didn't think I was actually out here surveying, did you?"

"You convinced me. Guess I was mistaken," said an irritated female voice.

Texie stepped out from a patch of dried-out brush about twenty feet away. Her pistol was cocked and pointed at them. From this distance, it was like looking down the barrel of a cannon. Alec gulped. He put his hands in the air. Randy followed likewise.

"Err, fancy meeting you here," Alec said. He tried to sound jaunty.

"It wasn't exactly an accident."

"You missed me?"

Texie did not look amused. In the least. In fact, her beautiful brown eyes seemed rather flat and overall disgusted with him. She soon confirmed that observation.

"I'm getting tired of coming after you, Malone. Maybe I should just shoot you and have done—save myself a whole boatload of future trouble." She nodded at Randy. "I suggest you move away from this outlaw directly, Mr. Grant."

Randy moved, all right. He plucked a metal canteen off the side of his saddle and flung it at her. By some stroke of luck, it struck true and clanged off her gun barrel. Randy launched himself at her like a coyote after a rabbit.

Before Alec could blink an eye, Randy and Texie had collided. They twisted this way and that in a desperate struggle over the gun. A lucky grab to one side and a shove, and Texie ended up sprawled on her shapely buttocks in the dirt in front of Alec. Randy gave a crooked grin and aimed the gun at her.

"Now, I can't let you capture my long lost pal, can I?"

Alec jumped in front of her. "Now, Randy, calm down. No one needs to shoot anybody. We can talk this misunderstanding out like calm, reasonable individuals."

"That's assuming I care a whit about being a calm, reasonable individual."

"Randy?" Texie repeated. She studied Randy's bony visage before revelation unfolded across her face. "Randy Andy Potlis . . . Potlik—"

"Potkalitski."

"That's it. Randy Andy Pot-licker. I thought you looked familiar. That cowlick of yours and that chunk missing out of your chin should have been dead giveaways."

Randy frowned. "It's not a chunk missing out of my chin. It's a dimple."

"Whatever it is, it's got you recognized from here to the Missouri River, you low-down, dirty skunk of a robber—taking old ladies' purses and kidnapping them hapless Chinese women!"

Randy didn't deny it. "That's not the half of what I've done, Miss Sheriff. You'd best be worried about yourself instead of them other women."

"Oh, I'm not worried. I'm going to throw you in jail."

Silence intruded like the deep, resonant tone of a gong. Randy's eyes were cold and flat. "I can't have that. Spurge, you need to move away from your 'friend' right now or you'll regret it."

Alec's heart turned to stone. "You're doing nothing to her, you hear me?"

Randy guffawed. "Never thought I'd see the day. You're sweet on her, aren't you, Spurge?"

"I should have known you would team up with him," Texie

said to Alec.

"Not at all. He's the one I told you about back in the jail cell. The sneaky, thieving partner."

"Really, Spurge?" Randy made a 'what the hell?' face, then gestured with the gun. "Do what I said. Move away from her. I can't allow her to leave this spot. You should know that. I'm not aiming to get caught."

"That's a bad idea, Randy. The Texas Rangers don't much cotton to peacemakers being shot up. They'll come after you in droves, track you down no matter how far you go or how long it takes."

Randy considered this for a breath. "You know, you're right. I don't want to risk that. Guess I'll have to find some other way to get free. Sorry about this, Spurge."

"Sorry about what?"

Randy lifted the gun from Alec's legs to his trunk. A shot exploded in a loud blast.

Something punched Alec in the chest. Hard.

Texie screamed. "No!"

Alec looked down at himself. A neat little hole tore right through the fabric and into his left shoulder. A fiery hot lance pierced through sinew and bone. He tried to cry out but couldn't seem to get enough breath. What happened . . . ?

Oh.

"Spurge! I'm sorry. I really am, but I had to!" Randy jammed the revolver into his pants. He surged forward to grab the palomino's reins and dashed out of sight.

"Bastard!" Alec bellowed.

Except that it came out more like a vague squeak. Alec made to go after him. After two steps, his knees gave out. He fell face first onto the hard-packed earth. Texie yelled something and tugged him over. He blinked slowly. Anxiety made her face tight and her words come quickly.

"You're going to be all right, Alec. You are going to be just fine, you hear me?"

She cast her gaze around, lower lip caught between her teeth. He tipped his head—a lot harder than it should have been—and saw what she was looking at. Dried up bunches of sagebrush and twisted, stunted pinyon pines. Dirt and rocks and a whole lot of nobody to help and nowhere much to go.

"Where's . . . the posse?"

"Moved on. I stayed behind to fetch you."

A spreading damp widened around the burning in his chest. He didn't want to look.

Texie took his face between her two warm hands. "We're going to make this all right, you hear me? And make sure that bushwhacking partner of yours gets what's coming to him. I promise you that, Alec." Her voice wavered.

She gave a gasp that sounded far too much like a sob and put her hand to her mouth as if to keep it inside.

Now he *knew* he was in trouble.

Chapter 18

Texie pushed down on Alec's good shoulder as he tried to rise.

"That bastard shot me." He sounded indignant. "He straight up shot me! Let me up. Can't have him get away. Not after I've found him at last . . ."

Texie held him down with one hand and tugged open his vest with the other. Bright red blood covered his shoulder and upper chest. It pulsed up like a bubbling spring with his heartbeat, but she couldn't pinpoint exactly where it came from. Her stomach rolled, and she flung herself away from him just in time to vomit into the sandy soil.

His mouth fell open. "The sight of blood makes you sick? Texie, you beat up people on a daily basis."

"It doesn't always bother me," she snapped. "Just when I see it on someone I care—I mean, someone I know."

Alec's sweaty face transformed with smug knowledge. "Uh-huh."

She wiped her mouth off on her sleeve. "Just be quiet, would you? You need to save your strength."

With fumbling fingers, she ripped the bandanna from around her neck and pressed it near the juncture of Alec's shoulder and armpit. It soaked up blood far too quickly. She needed something to wrap it with that would apply pressure. She tried to think around the screaming in her head. A belt. She reached for his belt buckle, a gigantic silver thing decorated with intricate vines and a rearing stallion. The leather belt was just as fancy, stamped with a matching vine edging.

"Darlin', you're being a bit forward, aren't you?"

"Quiet, you lecher."

She ignored his hisses and groans as she struggled to pass it under his back and through his armpit. Near as she could figure, the bullet wound pierced the skin two or so inches from his right armpit. She didn't think there was anything vital in that area, except for some blood vessels. If one was severed, he could bleed out under her fingers.

No, God, please don't let him die.

She cinched the belt as tight as she dared. A cold sweat popped over her entire body, but she forced down the resurgence of nausea by sheer willpower. An instant later, she threw herself to her feet and dashed a few hundred yards back to where she left Little Min tied to a heavy rock. She knotted her fingers in Little Min's reins.

"Come on, girl."

She had to get help for Alec. But how? They were at least a day's ride from town. Both groups of her posse were out here . . . somewhere. And while she could probably track them down without too much effort, no one there was any better than a spit and polish horse tender. She could do that much herself. So, to town it was. As long as she could control the bleeding, preventing infection was the biggest worry. She couldn't think that far ahead yet, though.

Getting Alec atop Little Min required as much exertion as

that time she'd had to steer two stinking drunk cowpokes into the jail after they'd soiled Carlene Gibson's floor, tables, and two of her working girls with excessive vomiting. To his credit, Alec tried to help, but his limbs didn't work right and he had all the strength of a day-old kitten.

Little Min waited patiently as she tugged and shoved Alec up to her back, though she did cast a few backward glances. Alec lay over Little Min's neck like a broken string puppet. She lashed the coil of rope around Ralph's neck and Alec's back, moving with such haste and panic that she burned her palms and sliced open cuts that soon slicked the rope with her blood.

Again with the blood.

She climbed up behind Alec. They rambled off at a trot. Behind them, Randy beat a hasty retreat. The idiot headed toward the sand flats where he would find all of nothing. And while Texie's gut burned with a need for vengeance, she put it aside. First things first.

Alec needed her.

She clung to Little Min's mane, arms wrapped around Alec's middle. Keeping them both mounted required continuous effort as they shifted this way and that over the rough terrain. Her arms strained and her chest seized with the effort.

Alec gave a contented sigh, eyes half closed. "This feels good. You against me . . . your Grand Tetons." He dissolved into what sounded like drunk giggles.

"Tetons? What are you on about?"

"It's French for breasts."

She snorted. "You are incorrigible."

"A leopard can't change his spots. And be honest. You wouldn't want him to if he could."

Her lips twitched upward. "You'll be showing those spots

on your deathbed, won't you?"

"Darn right." He paused. "That ain't today, though, darlin'." His voice sounded weak.

"Better not be."

"Yes, ma'am."

Their pace seemed agonizingly slow, though in reality, Little Min carried along at a decent speed despite the fact that she was overloaded with weight.

Texie stopped atop the first rise and retraced the path they had taken here, a circuitous route down around the bulge of a hill. A more direct path lay to the left, near a clump of three gnarled, thick dwarf oaks. She guided them toward it. Little Min's hooves clacked on the stones as they sped up through a bare, shale-littered patch. Straightway, then, they dove into the brush to follow an old game trail.

"Go, girl. Keep on!"

When she realized that Alec hadn't said anything in awhile, she spoke his name right into his ear and nudged his good shoulder. He didn't respond. She craned her neck to see his eyes closed and his face slack in unconsciousness.

The one time since they'd met that he had actually shut up. The silence was horrible. She increased pressure against his wound to keep that precious fluid where it belonged. He roused a bit from the pain, then slumped again moments afterward.

Soon—later? She could hardly tell—they burst through a wall of brush to see a clearing. More dwarf oaks stood to the right. Next to them, a fortuitous tumble of gray boulders formed a roof and two walls. Someone had exploited this natural feature by building a dwelling place there. Uneven pinyon pine branches formed walls to the front and back. The ones that hadn't broken and rotted away, that was. A well stood to the right made from heaps of good-sized stones. It was mostly intact, though the wooden frame from which dangled a half-broken bucket looked ready to collapse.

Texie froze in the saddle, senses sharp and wary. She scanned the house and noticed for the first time that two long agave poles lay propped against one of the walls. A pack made out of woven fibers hung suspended between them. Two blankets wadded into balls sat next to a shallow depression near the well. A basket with a geometrical black border rested against the well.

Indians!

Her spine straightened. Where were they? Careful examination revealed a gun barrel protruding from the trunk of one of the oaks pointed right at them. She fumbled for her gun, eyes never leaving the danger. Damn! It wasn't in its customary place in her holster. Where . . . ? Randy, that skunk.

A fringe of jet black hair appeared above the weapon. The gun barrel lowered. An Apache man in his thirties stepped out from behind the tree.

Texie recognized him at once. He was the Indian she and Alec had met a week or so ago when they were on the run from the gang and the Methodists. It seemed like months ago, so much had happened in the meantime.

"Yah ta hey," he said.

Hello.

"Help us," she blurted out. "Please."

He had the wide, square face of his people, the flat lips and smooth brown skin. His stoic expression gave nothing away. In the saddle in front of her, Alec gave a soft cry. The Apache took in the sight of him.

"Come," he told her. Then, in Apache, he said something low and urgent in the direction of the dwelling.

Two women emerged from behind it. Three children followed them, their eyes bright and curious. Texie recognized them from their first meeting.

She slipped down from the saddle, and all of a sudden, hands appeared all around her, helping her carry Alec to a smooth place on the ground in front of the house.

The women were both around Texie's age—she suspected they were sisters from the similar shape of their eyes. They tended to Alec at once, tearing his shirt all the way open. Pearl buttons popped off as they did so. Texie knelt and gathered them up. He'd fuss if they went missing for good. She tried not to look too closely at his wound lest she vomit again and humiliate herself in front of the toughest, most inscrutable people the West had ever seen.

Speaking of which, the man of the family grunted in her direction. He gestured toward the blankets, laid out in the open, dirty and probably crawling with fleas. Well, who was she to judge? He folded his knees and sat Indian-style. Not wanting to appear rude, she sat across from him.

The women murmured among themselves, then spoke to the boy and girl. The children scampered off to fetch supplies from one of the packs, then returned with armfuls of pouches, cloth, and an animal skin of water. Everyone seemed to know what they were doing. Except her.

Texie watched them from this position, safe from the sight of blood. After a while, she noticed that tears were coursing down her cheeks. She brushed them aside, the liquid hot on her fingers.

"You husband?" The man asked.

"Yes," she said for some insane reason. "I mean, no. He's . . ." How could she explain what Alec was to her? An annoyance, a companion through danger, a petty thief and a smart mouth, a handsome, lively, vibrant man who just couldn't be dying right now. He just *couldn't*.

She cleared her throat and shook herself a little. "I'm Texie Cortez." She pointed to the star on her chest, then to the east. "Sheriff of Abalone."

He pointed to himself. "Mangas." Then he gestured to the women. "Lenna. Kushala." She had no idea which was which, though.

She summoned up a weak, pathetic smile and tried to be brave.

Mangas eyed her.

The still air hung like curtains around them. Every now and again, Alec gave an agonized groan. The sound caused pangs in her heart, just like she'd read in those wretched but irresistible novels they sold in the women's corner of the general store.

After a while, Lenna and Kushala got up and left Alec's side. One of them mashed some plants with a mortar and pestle and smeared them all over his wound. The other bathed his chest clean of the blood, then tenderly washed his face.

Without a word to Texie, they got up and attended to making dinner. The girl child used a stick to dig a hole in the fire pit's ashes. Lenna, or at least the woman Texie had dubbed Lenna, carried over a clay pot filled with beans, tubers, and handfuls of what must have been seasoning leaves and placed it in the hole. The girl used her stick to work the embers around to cover the pot.

She took to peering unashamedly at Texie, then, and after scrutinizing her, she flashed a smile so fleeting that Texie wondered if she had imagined it.

Texie swallowed and nodded in Alec's direction. "Will he . . . do you think he will recover?"

She looked at Mangas. He shrugged but remained silent.

Texie's knee jittered as she sat at Alec's side. Alec had stilled, his face pale. She couldn't tell if his shallow breath came from sleep or unconsciousness. The sight of Randy's stupid face as he pulled the trigger and the great boom of the bullet speeding toward Alec replayed themselves in her mind like a rolling wheel that revolved over and over and flashed spokes. Rage sputtered and flared. She got to her feet and moved around the camp, unable to sit and fold her hands neatly like some sort of prayerful nun.

Mangas looked up from braiding a rope together from yucca fibers when she stopped in front of him. In a series of stumbling phrases and inadequate hand gestures, she communicated that she was leaving. He grunted in what she thought was the affirmative before saying something to the women, who seemed just as unimpressed. Then he went back to his task.

All right, then.

She emptied her saddlebag of whatever she thought the Apaches might need to care for Alec. A blanket, more rope, a hoof pick (to dig out the bullet, maybe?), a pen knife, biscuits, some string, and salve to cool the burning of insect bites. She cupped Alec's cheek in her hand and smoothed her thumb across the burgeoning stubble there. His eyelids fluttered. With a sigh, he came awake.

"Texie." He breathed her name low.

The sound of his voice made tears spring anew to her eyes. She blinked them away.

His eyes focused on her face, then dropped to take in the rest of her, all without moving his head more than an inch.

"You . . . get him, hear me?"

"Figured you would want that. Just get well while I'm gone, hear me?"

The corner of his mouth twitched. Holding her gaze seemed like too much effort. His eyelids sagged.

"You're beau'ful. Smart. Everythin' I want. Thought . . . you should know."

She leaned down and kissed his cheek where her hand had been and rested her forehead against his temple for a breath before straightening up. His eyes were closed again and his mouth slack.

She got up and took Little Min by the reins. Mangas watched her with mild curiosity. She explained that she had to chase down Alec's shooter because he was a bad man. No, not just a bad man, but a rotten to the core, worm-infested, foul apple.

He didn't react, even when she called out, "I'll be back as soon as I can!"

She had no idea whether he understood what she said. Then she twisted her hands into Little Min's wiry mane and vaulted into the saddle.

"Ya!" Texie cried and headed east after that bastard, Randy. And justice.

Chapter 19

Texie tried to summon forth the familiar sharp attention and all-consuming focus necessary to track Randy, but it took a lot more energy than Texie seemed to have available. At least until she put aside what may or may not be happening back at the Apache camp with Alec. She couldn't afford to worry about him now. Her life depended on it.

The day was warmer than usual for this time of year, and now the cloudless sky and the sun at full strength heated the ground around her like a cast iron skillet. Why, toss a smear of fat and a hastily formed tortilla on it and she'd be ready to eat. Eyes narrowed, she gripped the reins in claw-like hands. Beneath her, Little Min shifted and trotted, her compact form strong and steady, as usual.

Randy moved like a wild thing, panicked into scuffing the earth and breaking creosote branches. Sometimes, he turned his horse one way for a dozen yards, then backed up and took a different direction altogether. A disturbance in the sand showed that his horse had reared and lunged to the side. She reconstructed the event. Here, the slithering tracks of a rattler. There, the skid of hooves and Randy's boot prints as he dismounted to calm his horse. It must have involved some violence since his pocket watch and a handful of silver dollars littered the earth around the disturbed soil. She slipped the items into her saddlebags and took to the trail again. He had to know someone was following. Leastways, he acted like he did.

The sun dipped low on the horizon. Little Min breathed hard, not used to such exertion, but Texie pushed her on. When it became too dark to distinguish the small signs of tracking, she did not stop for the night like she would have in other situations. Instead, she followed instincts born of a childhood chasing frightened javelinas or mule deer across the desert, learning how to anticipate the movement of a creature running for its life. A man wasn't so different. Less smart in a lot of ways, even.

When the moon rose, she could again see the marks in the sandy earth and broken twigs—the horse manure and the spot where Randy had stopped for a little while to bandage an injury with part of his gingham shirt. He'd ripped the long sleeves off and left the rest wadded up on the ground, alongside his store of cooking utensils and a half dozen pouches filled with different soils he probably used to bolster his claims of working as a mining surveyor. Now, though, he needed to lighten the load and move quicker.

Grim satisfaction unfolded in her gut.

Texie's vision narrowed and the light from the glowing silver moon illuminated the brush and earth enough that she no longer cursed the darkness. Up and down, across—the soil turned even more sandy, and Little Min slowed as it dragged her hooves.

The sound of a horse breathing hard alerted Texie to Randy's presence before she saw him. She nudged Min's sides to speed her up. Together, they descended on Randy like the wrath of the Almighty. He had sprawled on the ground, bucked off by a frightened horse who even now tore off through the desert like a bird fleeing a net. The whites of Randy's eyes shone in the dark like lanterns and communicated one emotion. Desperation.

The flash of a gun. The explosion of a shot. Texie ducked alongside Little Min's neck and squeezed off a return shot. And another.

There was no talking this time. No bargaining or gloating. Just a quick and dirty scuffle for survival. One of Texie's bullets impacted the meat of his upper arm. Dust puffed out from the hit but he did not react otherwise. He tried to bang off some more shots, but the gun fell from his nerveless hand.

She sorely wanted to finish him off with a bullet to the brainpan but restrained herself. He scrabbled backward, crab walking, feeling around in the dirt for his weapon. She leapt forward and kicked it out of reach.

"You're under arrest." She sounded raw and cold, like a vengeful goddess.

He lunged at her in an uninspired move. She hopped out of reach and plucked the coil of rope off her saddle. With a frustrated cry, he flailed around, looking for something to use as a weapon. She let him wear himself out. Shortly, he did so and lay panting on the dimly lit earth, spent.

She pointed Miss Jennie right at the end of his crooked nose. "Get up. You're coming with me."

He didn't make a move. Instead, he just lay there and breathed. "Is he dead?"

Frozen needles pierced her chest. She spoke through a tight throat. "That's what you wanted, wasn't it?"

"S'pose so." Then he managed a grin. "Nah, not really. Never have been a very good shot. I wasn't expecting to hit him."

Her eyes burned. "Well, you did, you bastard. Right now, he's half dead in the dirt. All for what? Trusting you? Trying to get some vengeance?"

"He never did have the heart to do the hard stuff."

"Like murder?"

Randy heaved himself up to a sitting position. His right arm dangled, limp and loose. Blood darkened his sleeve, but she felt no nausea this time. Nothing but grim satisfaction.

He gave a miniscule shrug. "It ain't murder if it's for survival."

"Which it wasn't. He's a better man than you'll ever be."

Randy let out a harsh laugh. "Are you smitten, Miss Sheriff? He'll break your heart without a second thought."

She jammed the gun barrel in his neck with one hand and wound rope around his chest with the other. He didn't make a move, maybe because he feared she was looking for a reason to blow his head off. When he was trussed up like a Christmas goose, arms pinned to his side, she called his mount over. The little palomino had circled back after her initial fright, and she came readily. The hard pace had done the poor thing in. Sweat streaked her neck and shoulders and froth bubbled from her lips.

Texie plucked Randy's bandanna off his neck and used it to wipe the horse down as best she could. No more running for this girl.

She tugged Randy to his feet. After a fair amount of curses and threats to drag him along behind his horse, she got him over his horse's back, lying across the saddle. Texie looped the extra rope this way and that to secure him up there. It looked as uncomfortable as all hell. Good. When she finished, he raised his head and said, "He'll never stay with you, mark my words."

She grabbed a handful of Randy's messy brown mop and yanked his head up further. "Shut that clap trap of yours."

Doleful dark eyes. A smudged, sun-browned face and a sweat-soaked odor that could have felled a rhinoceros from fifty yards. Luckily for her, she had a high tolerance for stinky men after arresting a number of poorly bathed cowpokes. She tied Randy's soaked bandanna around his arm wound. The bullet had gone clean through and the wound was already clotting.

"I didn't mean it. You tell him that, if he lives long enough. I did him wrong, I know that. But I never wanted him gone for good."

"You sure I'm the one in love with him?"

He shut up good and proper after that.

She should have stopped for what remained of the night. It would have saved her listening to Randy's all-too-content snores on one hand and his grunts and complaints on the other. And from a considerable amount of eye strain as she picked out their destination in the dark, as well as a few panicked stops as she tried to figure out whether she'd led them off the trail or not. Once or twice, she fell asleep with her eyes open and snapped awake with no memory of the immediate past.

But stopping seemed too close to giving up, so she kept at it. Her thoughts ran helter skelter around Alec, Alec, Alec, that force of nature who occupied such a space in her life. Her mind. Her . . . heart.

Dawn came cold and slow, the slide of thick molasses from a jar. With the better light, she could see the direct route to the Apaches' camp. Little Min stumbled with weariness, and

Randy's palomino hung her head and plodded on in misery, but Texie couldn't let them rest yet.

Randy was quiet. Passed out, maybe? Dead from that wound? She probably should care more about that.

On they went through the brush and across the sand flats. Jackrabbits rustled the brush and red-tailed hawks chased one another in a whirling, squawking dance.

Then, a familiar stand of dwarf oaks, crashing through the brush—exhilaration! The boulder house stood gray and half-hidden in the brush.

And empty.

Where were the Apaches? Off hunting, maybe. But what about the children? Their baskets and blankets were gone, the cook fire covered with dirt.

No.

She searched the ground for tracks, clues, anything.

"Mangas!"

They wouldn't have taken Alec along with them. Maybe they didn't need to. Maybe he up and died in the night and they buried him—

"They moved on, darlin'."

She spun around. Alec leaned against the doorway of the boulder house. His hair was wet, his white shirt unbuttoned halfway down his chest. With a wet bandanna, he dabbed at a pink, fist-sized bloodstain over his shoulder.

He was upright. *Alive.*

"How . . . ?"

She flew into his arms and jammed her lips against his for a passionate kiss. Tears coursed down her face. Her hands traveled up the smooth muscles of his back. Then, somehow, they ended up on his cheeks, their faces too close. His skin felt warm and looked a little pale. But his eyes shone brightly. She drew back.

"Don't ever do that to me again," she ordered shakily. "Don't leave me like that, you bastard. I want you—"

She broke off when she realized the crazy words that tumbled out of her mouth. He pulled her against the unwounded side of his chest. She clung to him like a battered, broken thing. He smelled so good, so right, like everything she'd ever desired.

His vocal cords rumbled against her hair. "I'm pleased to see you, too. And I want you as well, in case you didn't know. Enough to—"

"Don't say it! I don't want to hear any bullshit promises. I'm just happy you're all right."

He smiled. "I'm happy as well. Let me show you how much."

Then he kissed her, soft and perfect, his breath sweet, their bodies pressed together, and sensations ran riot over her and blotted out the sun and sky and the very earth beneath her feet. It must have been too much for Alec because after a couple of moments, he had to lean against the doorpost or fall down.

Turns out that Alec had woken up an hour or so after she took off. The Apaches poured some sort of wretched agave alcohol down his throat and he perked right up.

"They seemed surprised at that," he commented.

The two of them sat against a wall of the boulder house so that Alec could recover himself. His left arm draped across her, keeping her close. She didn't want to admit how much she liked the feel of him there against her.

"You mean to tell me that a little booze replaced all that lost blood?"

"I s'pose so. I'm so strong and virile that nothing can keep me down for long."

She side-eyed him. "You sure you didn't faint from the pain?"

"Faint is such an . . . inadequate term. I'm certain I was inches from expiring. Delirious. Possibly even comatose."

She kissed his neck, drawing a low noise of pleasure from him.

"All I know is that I've never been as happy to see a walkin', talkin' con artist."

"You seem to be the only one. The Indians up and took off before dawn without even a fare thee well. They nudged me awake, shoved a canteen of water at me, and left."

She sat up and looked him over. "You're really all right?"

"My bones are creaking. My shoulder hurts like the devil. And I'm a little dizzy. But I'm good. My shirt, on the other hand, is all ripped to hell and stained with blood. Do you know how much I paid for that thing?"

"Too much, I'm sure." She reached into her breast pocket and dug out his pearl buttons.

He beamed. "You know how to win a fellow's heart."

"Ain't that nice?" came a muffled voice from the lump on the back of the palomino some two dozen feet off. "Now get me down afore my guts leak out my head."

Alec's eyes widened. "Is that . . . ?"

She'd forgotten all about Randy.

"Yep. Sadly, he's still alive."

"Hey!"

"You did shoot her number-one man," Alec piped up with surprisingly good humor.

She raised her eyebrows at him. "You seem awfully forgiving."

"Oh, I ain't no saint, darlin'. I still mean to get my pound of flesh outta him. But I'm also grateful. I woulda never come here and met you if it hadn't have been for that slippery snake."

She smiled back and squeezed his hand. They had lots to do now that Alec was all right. Arrests to make, wounds to tend, some decent meals to have, and long-needed baths to soak in. But for now, she just sat and stared at his precious face, and she couldn't honestly remember a time when she'd felt so happy.

Chapter 20

When Alec rode into the posse's camp accompanied by Texie and that low-down dirty traitor, Randy, Roger confronted them first. He sat atop a white, pink-eyed mare, his leg curled around the saddle horn in such a way that his ballooned-up injured ankle could rest.

"Sheriff!" he crowed at a volume that made a flurry of doves burst from a nearby bush.

Alec, who rode behind Texie on Little Min, felt her wince.

"Quiet!" she hissed. "The Bully Flamencos could be around any corner!"

Her chastisement didn't work, though, because by that time, everyone else had spotted them. Grins broke out all around and the posse surrounded them in a matter of moments. Questions came from everywhere at once.

"What's that bandage on your shoulder, Mr. Malone? You look mighty pale, you do."

"Hey! Don't that rump belongs to Mr. Grant? What's he doing all tied up over the back of this here filly?"

"Glad you're here, Sheriff. Milo done got us lost—"

"That ain't true!" Milo squawked.

Texie got down off Little Min, pushed between the loudest of the two, Milo and Jack Daw, and harangued at them to shut up.

Alec watched her. In fact, he couldn't take his eyes off her. Fury and justice radiated from her blazing brown eyes. His eyes fixed on her luscious red lips, the most delicious he'd ever tasted. He'd never seen the likes of her. Smart, beautiful, strong, and once in a blue moon, sweet, too.

In the midst of all the tumult, she glanced over at him, her eyebrows raised in such a way that he realized that his admiration was showing on his face. He winked and pursed his lips into a kiss.

Her lips quirked up in response, though half a heartbeat later, she laid into Jack, this time for the shoddy job he'd done covering their tracks.

Jack's feathers ruffled. "But how were you gonna find us if we didn't leave no tracks?"

"You should have been worrying more about getting ambushed by the outlaws. Like I said, I can find you whenever I want to," Texie replied.

Randy lifted his head. "Let me down offa this horse! This is cruel and unusual punishment!"

Alec supposed it was. Randy had been tied up and slung over the back of his horse for about fifteen hours now, except for a brief space to do his business and gnaw on a piece of jerky that Texie gave him for dinner.

When no one responded to his demand, Randy craned his neck at Alec. "Have pity, Spurge! Talk to her, would ya?"

He looked downright desperate, his face all flushed and his eyes wild. Alec sneered in response. That motion caused him to move his chest somehow because a sharp pang dug into his wounded shoulder. He hissed in pain.

All the hullaballoo settled down after about ten minutes.

Cookie doled out some cold griddle cakes he'd fried up this morning, and the lot of them hunkered under the scant shade of a cluster of pinyon pines, spread out a map, and plotted where to head next.

Alec didn't join in but instead propped himself up against a boulder and sipped on Milo's special concoction, a mixture of "health and virility-inducing" rotgut so tart that it made his eyes cross. The ride here and the warmth of the day, not to mention the recent blood loss, made him dizzy and weak.

Texie glanced at him with concern. He tried to perk up. She came over and sat next to him. Their shoulders joined, and her hand snaked up to hold his.

Milo and Jack pulled Randy off the back of his horse to rest on his side in the dirt. Jack secured his ropes well.

Texie nodded at him. "Why does he call you Spurge? Alec isn't your real name?"

"No, it is. Sort of. My entire name is Alexander Spurgeon Malone."

"Spurgeon. Like the fish?"

"That's a sturgeon. Like the famous Word of God preacher, Charles Spurgeon."

She tipped her chin. "I've heard of him. Guess it fits that you'd be named after someone who talks for a living."

He nuzzled her cheek and spoke low in her ear. "Oh, I can do more than that with this mouth of mine. I assure you."

She blushed and moved to stand up.

"Now don't go—"

"I'd stay if I could. Got to see to these fellows."

Six of them were thick in the 'where do we go next' argument. Alec sighed in resignation. Texie's fingers brushed his cheek. He tried to pay attention to the argument, which had devolved into name calling by this point, but he closed his eyes to rest them for a moment.

When he opened them again, it was to see Texie hunkered down in front of him, a crooked grin at the corner of her lips.

"Sorry to wake you."

"I wasn't sleeping."

"Uh-huh."

"We got it figured out. Finally. We're headed over thataway." Texie gestured west. "Milo thinks he saw some smoke out of that spyglass of his. Most of us are willing to risk it."

Alec felt like a dishrag that had been scrubbed across a filthy floor, soaked in lye soap, and smacked across a boulder fifty or sixty times. But at least he was less likely to faint after resting for a spell.

Texie got to her feet and extended a hand. "Will you accept help from a lady?"

He took her hand. "I'll accept a lot more than that, if you're offering."

Her eyes lit with amusement. She drew a breath to respond and froze.

"Where's Pot-licker?" Her voice bit like a rattlesnake.

The rest of the posse looked at her with slack jaws. Disturbed sand marked the place where he had been lying just a few moments ago.

Cookie spoke up. "Marvin took him to take a shi—poop, ma'am."

"That was a good ten minutes ago!" she exclaimed. "How in the hell long does he need?"

The men exchanged glances. Milo snickered. "Depends on whether he had somma Cookie's coffee or not."

At that moment, Marvin staggered from the bush. His

battered old hat sat askew on his head and a fist-sized mark reddened his left cheekbone.

"Dammit, he absquatulated!" Texie cried.

Alec caught his stomach mid-drop. "He ran off?"

"That's what I said!"

It turned out that Randy had cracked Marvin on the noggin and absconded into the great unknown. Once Marvin's eyes uncrossed, Alec seized him by the arms.

"Where did he go?"

"Thataway." Marvin pointed east.

Rage restored Alec's vigor. He flew to Ralph and untied his leads. When he knotted his fingers in Ralph's mane to haul himself to his back, he noticed Texie right next to him. Her face was still . . . carefully blank.

"What are you doing?"

"I'm going after him, of course!"

"Randy's headed east. We're here to go after the gang—that means west."

Alec set his jaw. "I'm not letting him get away, not again. Not when he's so close."

Texie's eyes hardened. "Oh. I see. It never was about the gang for you, was it? It was always about Randy."

The tone of her voice made something twist low in his gut. "Now darlin', that's not the case at all. But I've been chasing that rascal for three years, and if I don't go now, he'll be gone again. Don't worry. I'll be back. I promise." He leaned in for a quick peck on the cheek.

She said nothing and stepped out of his way.

He glanced back just before disappearing down the game trail. She stood in the same spot, watching him go with a forlorn look on her face.

The game trail—Randy's trail—split in half after less than a mile. Alec debated continuing to follow it east, toward town. If Randy had a brain inside that hard head of his, he would head that way. Except that Randy didn't have even a third of a brain when he smelled money. Alec took the trail that headed west, toward the canyons where the gang was likely holed up.

He guided Ralph through the brush for two hours without seeing another soul. The vegetation had thickened here, tall grass and weeds and fat stubby bushes with tiny, sharp-edged leaves that snagged his shirt and trousers. The game trail had petered out a while back, and he'd been navigating based on his instincts. Hills folded one into another up ahead, beyond which lay the bare, forbidding peaks of the Guadalupes. He proceeded carefully, keeping his head down and his mouth shut. Yes, Texie would be proud of how quiet and smart he was. He congratulated himself.

A pistol cocked behind him.

"I'd git on down from that mule if I was you," advised an unfamiliar male voice. "And do it slowly cuz I got myself a mean trigger finger."

Chapter 21

A lec did what the stranger said. He dismounted Ralph without making any sudden movements and raised his hands.

"Now whath we got here, Murl?" lisped a lazy male voice.

Two scraggly-looking outlaws glanced at one another. Alec could smell their rancid stink from eight feet away. The one with the gun on him grinned wide enough to display a single snaggly tooth. That's what made his voice come out with a slobber-spraying lisp. Combined with his crossed eyes, it made his appearance both horrible and disturbing. Where should one look without offending him? Alec settled on the tip of his pockmarked nose.

"A walking corpse, says I," mumbled Murl. He smiled with one corner of his mouth. The other side of his mouth—heck, the whole right side of his face—drooped, identifying him as a stroke victim. Alec found it hard to dredge up sympathy for the wretch.

"Gentlemen!" He plastered a fake smile on his face. "What good luck it is to find you at last!"

The first outlaw scrunched up his face in confusion. "You looking to find uth? Usss," he clarified.

"Yes, indeed, my good fellows. I am here to meet with the

esteemed Mr. Snarly Pete. I have information he will find invaluable—and an irresistible proposition as well."

"Uh, whut?"

"An idea, Chickie," slurred Murl. His one perfectly functioning eye bored into Alec. "We don't let just anyone waltz into our hideaway. Convince us."

"I'm afraid that my news is for the ears of the master alone. Why, even hearing what I have to say puts you in terrible danger!" He bent closer and said in a loud whisper, "Snarly Pete might have you killed."

Murl and Chickie jerked backward as one, their eyes wide.

"Thath impor-imp-th . . . serious?" Chickie warbled.

"Indeed."

Chickie's gnarled eyebrows drew together as he shot a frustrated glare at his partner. "Dammit all to hell. Thith mean I cain't shoot him?"

"Not yet, Chickie. Maybe soon."

"Err . . . that would be a terrible error in judgement. You see, I come by way of Mrs. Carlene Gibson over at the Desert Rose. She would be mighty unhappy were you to shoot me. And from what I hear, her unhappiness is the same as Snarly Pete's."

Murl and Chickie looked at one another.

"How're we gonna make sure he's not a lawman?" Chickie whined. "SP said he'd kill us good iffin we gave away our hidin' place. 'Member he said that, Murl?"

"I 'member."

Murl studied Alec, his seamed lips pursed as he puzzled over what to do next. Alec could practically hear the rusted, broken down wheels in his head turning.

"You could ask me the password." Alec mustered the most

helpful tone he could.

Murl's eye lit up. "That's a damn fine ideer! Ain't it, Chickie?"

Chickie motioned with the gun. "Have at it."

"Pink puppies."

The two of them goggled at him. An Arctic chill blasted Alec's spine. Carlene wouldn't have double-crossed him, would she?

"Talk about a dithappointment." Chickie holstered his weapon. "Come on, fanthy panth." He motioned for Alec to get ahead of them.

Alec tried not to stumble as relief weakened his limbs.

"You walk," commanded Murl. "We ride."

Chickie clambered onto Ralph's back. Ralph didn't much like double the weight and put up a fuss by snorting and snapping at Chickie's left ankle. He ripped out a hunk of Chickie's canvas britches. Murl tried to bat the deadly teeth away, but as he did this with his stroke-weakened arm, it was more like flinging about a roll of sausage.

Alec stepped in. After some sweet talking and a nubbin of jerky, Ralph became more cooperative. They took off, crashing through the brush like buffalo, heedless of any sort of path. Alec trailed them, but soon, in order to keep up, he had to knot his fingers in Ralph's wiry tail. The mule then proceeded to drag him along for a good hour as they wound through the chaparral. At length, they came to a game trail that crossed a creek and headed up the mountain fold.

The going was steep. Sweat coursed down Alec's neck and back, soiling what was left of his expensive shirt and bending his winged collar so that it stuck out on either side like horns. Added to the tears and snags from bumbling through the brush, he completed the picture of a vagabond. Oh, to return to civilization and proper male attire!

They topped a rise and descended through a grove of old cedars and oaks. He sniffed a whiff of cook smoke and heard the murmur of men's voices.

Chickie palmed his gun and motioned for Alec to go ahead of Ralph with an order of, "Raith them hands, Mithter."

Alec hastened to obey. Moments later, they entered a camp ringed by granite cliffs. Tents and lean-tos sat everywhere. Several dozen men lounged about playing cards, smoking cigars, or jawing. They observed Alec and his captors with interest.

An earthen lodge with a long, crooked porch dominated the right-hand corner of the space. On that porch stood a little twig of a man, old and gnarled but wearing a ten-gallon cowboy hat with eagle feathers stuck in the brim. Despite his unimpressive physical dimensions, he had a presence about him that held Alec's attention. This would be Snarly Pete.

"What do we have here?" the man hollered.

"This feller wanth to meet with you, Mithter Pete."

"Bring 'im on over! I do like me visitors."

Snarly Pete sounded cheerful in a demented sort of way. Like wolves scenting their prey, the other men sniffed and gathered around Alec. They followed the three of them as they approached Snarly Pete. Alec tried not to think about how eagerly they would rip his throat out if he gave them cause.

"Sir." Alec nodded and groveled in what he hoped was a respectful manner. "I'm here courtesy of Mrs. Carlene Gibson. She has particular affection for you, Mr. Pete."

Snarly Pete smiled to reveal a plug of chewing tobacco tucked in his cheek. A brown line of tobacco juice oozed out of it. He coughed and spat an arc of the fluid within inches of Alec's

$100 boots. He forced himself not to yell, dance aside, or vomit at the foulness of it.

"Well, now, I'm mighty fond of her, too. If you know what I mean." He winked and made a lewd pumping gesture with his hips. The ruffians around cackled and snorted. "Before we get to conversatin' I need to be sure I don't have to kill you right away."

"He gave uth the right words, bosth," Chickie hastened to say.

Snarly Pete's eyes reminded Alec of coal dust. Flaky, black, and reflectionless. The downturned lips that gave him his moniker stayed that way for a few agonizing beats of Alec's heart. Then they softened.

"Glad to hear that Mrs. Carlene did me good. Guess you're going to live out the day, Mister . . . ?"

Alec reached out to shake Snarly Pete's wrinkled, wiry paw. "Alec Malone at your service."

"Well, have yourself a sit." Snarly Pete gestured at the two rocking chairs on the makeshift porch. He spoke to a hunch-backed fellow who emerged from the shadows. "Horace, bring us some cool lemonade, will ya?"

"We ain't got none of that, Boss. We do got some Tejas Lightning."

Snarly shucked off his hat and scratched his thinning pate. "Seems awful early for that and sacrilegious too, on account of it bein' Sunday, but what the hell. Bring them madeleines, too."

"All ate up, Boss."

"Dammit, Horace. First you run out of lemonade and now there's no more of my favorite dainties. What kind of a quartermaster are you?"

Horace scuttled over like a cockroach.

"I was gonna make some up yesterday, Boss. But we runned outta butter."

Snarly Pete grabbed the megaphone next to his chair and bellowed into it. "Anders! Wardell! Git over here!"

Anders and Wardell immediately stopped stringing up their wet laundry and dashed over to cower in front of Pete, whose tiny hard eyes looked even tinier and harder as he stared them down.

"Why didn't you get butter on the last supply run like I told you to?"

Anders licked his lips like a nervous lizard. "We tried, Boss. But they was out of it!"

Snarly Pete looked at Wardell. "And what do you have to say for yourself?"

"He's telling the truth, I swear!"

Snarly Pete jumped to his feet and whipped out a gigantic serrated knife that resembled a sword. "You two idiots shoulda gone on to the next town, then! You know I need my madeleines! Now get in the pig pen before I stick you in the eyeballs!"

Anders and Wardell ran over to the pig pen like they were chased by six angry bulls and a ball of lightning. A sow the size of a donkey squealed in outrage when they jumped in the mud puddle and splashed around like . . . well, like pigs in shit.

Horace came out bearing a tray with two smudged, cloudy glasses full of brown liquid.

Snarly Pete chortled at the sight that Anders and Wardell presented then chugged his glass. "Yeehaw!"

Alec took a sip gingerly. Then he resisted the impulse to run over and drown his tongue in the creek on account of the fact that it was on fire. He managed to stay in his rocking chair, though, and eventually, his eyesight cleared. Snarly Pete was going on about the first time he saw Carlene and how he had to have her even though she charged him double on account of his weirdly forked . . . Alec tried to pay attention, then wished he hadn't.

When Snarly Pete finished his story, he gave a happy sigh. "So, what can I do you for, young feller? I know you didn't come all the way out here to watch a couple of morons wallow around in the mud."

Said morons seemed intent on accomplishing this task with a fervor and attention to detail that had lacked on their butter-finding mission. Wardell leaped on Anders and shoved his head into the ground. Flailing and gurgling ensued.

Alec tried to answer Snarly Pete, but his voice came out as a hoarse whisper. This must have been on account of the fact that he couldn't feel his throat after that drink. He tried again.

"Well, sir. I have come with an urgent warning about a man who is on his way here as we speak, Randy Potkalitski. He is a damn deceiver, a dastardly devil, a demented debaucher—"

Snarly Pete's wiry eyebrows climbed halfway up his forehead. Perhaps Alec *was* laying it on a little thick.

"Anyhow, this malcontent means to foist his foul self upon you and your fellows, to join your gang, and then, just when you trust him, steal your loot and turn you over to the law for a hefty reward."

Snarly Pete didn't look as mortified as Alec would have liked. In fact, he didn't look mortified at all. He leaned in, his rickety old rocking chair squeaking, and trapped Alec with his beady eyes like a bug under glass.

"Now, young feller, you know that ain't the truth, don't you?"

Alec gulped. "I know that he's a dirty sneak who will rob you as soon as look at you."

"You forget where you are, boy? That's a good thing hereabouts. Though I personally don't much likes it when someone such as yourself lies to me. It's aggravatin', it is."

He started digging at his rocking chair with his knife. His incredibly huge knife that had probably been sharpened the other day. Or even this morning. "What is it you want with old Randy now?"

Alec thought twice. Lying seemed like a dangerous option. But that had never stopped him before. "It's a complicated situation, sir. A family matter that involves a female in a delicate condition, if you know what I mean."

Snarly Pete twisted the knife, and a chunk of wood the size of Alec's knuckle popped out. "Tell me more."

"He's married to my sister, Evangeline. Got her with child again. That's six times in as many years! But he skipped out on her, and I mean to see that he owns up to his responsibilities."

"Ah. Makes sense. Had me a bunch of sisters myself. They helped me become the ladies' man I am today, even despite the forked . . ."

Under normal circumstances, Alec would have been curious about the appearance of this appendage. But considering what the rest of Snarly Pete looked like, he was certain it would pollute his imagination.

"Anywhatways. I know all about Randy Potkalitski. I s'pose were I to have some common decency, I'd help you outta the goodness of my heart. Problem with that is I don't got no common decency. I'll tell you this, though. He's already a member of the Bully Flamencos."

Alec sat up straight. "He's here?"

"Mebbe. Mebbe not. I don't much like selling out my gang members. Leastways, not without a good reason."

Alec thought fast. "How about if I offer you something downright irresistible?"

"Feller, Miss Carlene is a long ways from here. I can't think of anythin' as irresistible as her."

"What about a crate of madeleines made by the finest pastry chef in Dallas?"

Snarly Pete let out a guffaw that sounded like a strangled goose's honk. "You're a smart feller, ain't ya? Know just how to offer a man what he likes."

"I try."

"I respect that. I do. But here's the thing. You gotta know a little something about the gang. And that's this. We are a modern bunch of fellers. We have vision. And some of us even got some brains in our heads. Why, we're expanding. All over the West. Even charging a license fee. That ole Randy feller made it all the way to be second in command in our Col-o-rado Regional Office. Does a right fine job of it, too. Stole a bunch o' gold dust off the miners on Cripple Creek, ran some whorehouses out of Leadville, bribed some fat cat politicians. I've got to say, he right impressed me. And that, sonny, ain't easy to do."

Alec admitted, "He always was an enterprising fellow." With other people's money.

"Now I ain't seen his like for a good, oh, ten months now, back in Col-o-rado. 'Course, that ain't where he is now—"

At that moment, the door behind them burst open and three men strode out, not pausing at the porch to acknowledge Snarly Pete. They each wore black, from head to toe.

"Is it time, Brother John Henry?" Snarly Pete called after

them.

John Henry said over his shoulder, "It is indeed, Brother Peter. The word of the Lord is come!" He held up his worn copy of the Good Book. His two lackeys scurried after him.

The Methodists.

Alec had hoped, perhaps uncharitably, that they had either been chased off to Acapulco or had met their demise at the hands of the gang.

John Henry marched to the center of camp under the boughs of a gigantic aged oak tree. His lackeys, Wilbur Joe and his dimwitted brother, Bilbo Joe, rushed about arranging stumps and camp chairs for the audience. John Henry himself yanked a rustic pulpit out from behind the tree and set to arranging his crumpled papers on it. Next, he hung his stovetop hat from a conveniently placed withered branch. He licked both palms and smoothed down his unruly hair.

The shock of their appearance abated enough that Alec remembered what Snarly Pete had been about to say. He cleared his throat. "You were saying that Randy Potkalitski isn't in Colorado now, Mr. Pete?"

Snarly Pete surged out of his rocker. "We'll talk about that later, young feller. Right now, it's time for some good ole-fashioned preachin'!"

When Alec did not immediately spring out of his seat, Snarly Pete's beady eyes glittered. "You're coming, ain't you?"

"Of course!" he cried with false heartiness and followed with quick steps.

Chapter 22

Alec took a seat next to Snarly Pete, who sat in the front row. From his pulpit, John Henry glanced up at them. When he recognized Alec, his eyes narrowed, then lit like the fires of Hades. If looks could kill, Alec would have found himself skinned alive and boiled in Cookie's pot.

"Ring forth the bells of salvation!" John Henry hollered across camp.

One of the nearby outlaws who was stirring a giant iron pot of something over a fire rang the dinner bell like an enthusiastic Quasimodo.

Wilbur Joe broke out his harmonica and hummed a tune while Bilbo Joe took to warbling the hymn *Shall We Gather at the River?* as men streamed over to take their seats. Three gents seated directly behind Alec and Snarly continued their argument about the merits of city prostitutes versus small-town prostitutes—including colorful anecdotes of inventive lewd practices—until Snarly snapped, "Shaddap, you heathens!"

Snarly had a surprisingly robust singing voice for one so small. In respect, he took off his sweat- and dirt-stained hat to reveal a thinning oily mass of black hair plastered to his lumpy head.

"Git on over here!" Snarly Pete bellowed at the remaining

stragglers.

They dragged themselves over with a noticeable lack of piety. John Henry motioned to Bilbo Joe, who let fly with the next hymn.

Bringing in the Sheaves
Bringing in the Sheaves
We shall come rejoicing
Bringing in the Sheaves . . .

Alec added his voice to that of the scattered wheezing of the outlaws and the loud, rousing tones of Snarly Pete. Tears sparkled in the old reprobate's eyes. He took out a red paisley bandana and dabbed at his nose like a debutante.

John Henry slapped his Bible down on the pulpit where it made a resounding thud. Then he went to town, leading a twenty-minute-long prayer in which he begged for forgiveness and railed about the world's injustices. Next, he launched into the sermon. Alec had a hard time following it due to the mesmerizing sight of the spittle flying from John Henry's impassioned mouth. There was a lot of damnation and hellfire and finger pointing. John Henry accused his congregation for they way they broke each and every one of the Ten Commandments gleefully and without abandon. He described the many and varied tortures of hell, some of which, like the flaming hot branding iron shoved up one's bumhole, made Alec cringe and squirm in his chair.

Snarly Pete listened with rapt attention to John Henry's castigation. He didn't seem offended at the recitation of the sins that he, as the evil leader of a gang of ruffians, committed regularly.

Horace had taken a place on the stump on the other side of Alec. Alec inclined his head and said in a low voice, "Those preachers carry on like this all the time? Snarly Pete doesn't object?"

Horace sighed. "Yessir, they does. Don't seem to fear getting their heads split or nothin'. Boss man loves his Sunday meetings, he does."

"Shh!" Snarly Pete hissed.

By the time the sermon ended, Alec's ass had long since gone numb. Snarly Pete leapt up with a gleam in his piggy eyes.

"Weeeeeee hawww! Now's it's time for some rejoicin'!"

The rest of the outlaws' soft snores and dejected sighs ended under a barrage of cheers. Four outlaws burst out of one of the larger tents and came skipping over to the service. Alec gaped. They wore flour-sack dresses, handkerchiefs tied around the tops of their heads in Russian babushka style, and necklaces fashioned out of sardine-can lids.

Wilbur Joe let fly with a sprightly Spanish-sounding tune, and the four "ladies" set their chins, snapped their fingers, and danced in stomping, grunting whirls.

Alec gawped. "What are they doing?"

Snarly Pete managed to hear him over the sound of his own hooting and clapping. "Why, it's the flamenco, young feller! Bully style!"

Without a wooden floor to clack their heels on, the dancing created a lot of shuffling and kicking. Little clouds of dust rose up. The occasional bursts of *Arriba! Arriba!* interrupted the harmonica tunes. John Henry's mean, craggy face softened an iota. He even clapped his hands to the rhythm.

Snarly Pete grabbed one of the "women" and twirled her around, creating high and shrieking peals of laughter.

Down in El Paso, Alec had attended a peyote smoking session that involved disturbing visions of a twelve-foot tall rabbit. That experience seemed less bizarre than this one. But when in Rome . . .

He kicked up his heels and stamped this way and that. Alec prided himself at his skill with east-coast polkas and the southern waltzes—both of which had ended numerous times in rather lusty encounters with his dance partners—but he looked like a damn fool doing the flamenco.

Not that it mattered. It's not like any woman (beautiful, remote, righteous Texie) was watching.

Hollers, kicks, and spontaneous Russian squat dances ensued. Bilbo Joe flung his arms heavenward and his eyes rolled back in his head. Incomprehensible gibberish flowed from his lips.

"The Holy Spirit has descended!" John Henry announced.

Bilbo Joe spoke in tongues, or just blathered like an idiot—Alec had never been able to discern the two—until he seized up, jittered a bit, and collapsed into Wilbur Joe's arms. Wilbur Joe dragged him away from the stomping feet and smacked his face until he roused.

The whole thing lasted far too long as far as Alec was concerned. But it ended abruptly when someone held up a freshly opened bottle of whiskey.

Anders and Wardell, covered now in dried flakes of black mud, joined the fray, too.

Snarly Pete sank down on a stump, breathing hard. "Hoooey damn! That did a body good!"

Alec sat next to him. Fresh sweat dampened his once-pristine shirt anew, but at this point, he had pretty much decided to burn the thing. Being a fancy dude did not come easily out here.

"That was a singular experience, Mr. Pete," Alec declared.

"Singular indeed! Why, that makes a young fellow like me wish he could stay longer. It's a crying shame, but time is of the essence. My dear sister Evangeline is about to bust any day now, you know, and once she does, she needs a man about. I'd appreciate it if I could get ahold of that Randy. I happen to know that he's on his way here as we speak."

"Is that so?"

"It is, I solemnly swear."

"Yes, madeleines sound awful dee-lish-us about now," Snarly reflected. "You get me those and Randy's all yours. Hell, I can always get me a new lieutenant bad man, can't I?"

"But that will take me weeks to get there and back. My sister—"

"Probably doesn't exist. Now I know you want that feller, but I've got to get mine. And I'm thinking . . . well, I'm thinking that in addition to them sweets, I'd like a pretty woman by the name of Madeline."

"You . . . want me to give you a woman, too?"

Snarly Pete's eyes narrowed. "That ain't too much to ask, now is it? Since I'll be turnin' over one of my own, after all."

"Of course not," Alec asserted weakly.

Now why in the hell hadn't he offered something easier and more accessible? Like, say, sixteen angels dancing on the head of a pin?

Snarly Pete looked at him expectantly.

"You are one shrewd negotiator, Mr. Pete."

Snarly Pete spread his lips in a rictus of a smile so demented that it made pins and needles crawl up Alec's back.

"'Course, that's assuming he meets us here like we agreed—"

A blast went off.

Gunfire!

Bullets screamed past him and Snarly Pete. Rapid *pfft-pfft-pffts* smacked into the heavy tree limb directly behind them. Wood chips sprayed out. Alec flung himself to the ground and searched the brush-covered hills around them. Another explosion of gunfire erupted. The flash of multiple ignitions revealed a handful of assailants.

The posse.

Dammit all.

Chapter 23

"Double dammit and a slice of cherry pie," Texie proclaimed.

Roger's head popped up from where he had been concealed behind a rock outcropping fifty yards off. He looked hopeful. "Cherry pie?"

"Not now, you dimwit. Get back to shootin'!"

He frowned but did what she asked.

A barrage of gunfire sounded from across the canyon where Rancho and his crew had staked out positions. Her posse and Rancho's had coordinated their assaults from different angles, and they were both putting on a damn fine show of it.

Shouts went up from a few hundred yards below them. Several dozen outlaws ran to and fro, panicked. Moments before, they had been dancing like a pack of idiots—some of whom had been dressed like women.

She gritted her teeth. "I'll give you something to dance about."

With a squint, she aimed her pistol at the ground next to a fat fellow in a dress. She squeezed the trigger. The dirt erupted into a little dust devil at his right foot. He gave a high shriek, lifted his knees like a frightened ostrich, and took off running. He zigzagged out of her line of sight.

Texie gave a loud whistle. When she got her posse's attention, she motioned down the hill. The chaos generated by their attack wasn't going to last forever, and she would just as soon keep her men from getting their heads shot off. Like cats hunting mice, they hunkered down and crept forward, eyes fixed on the action in the camp.

Rancho's posse continued to make their way into the camp from opposite Texie and her men. Gunshots pinged in different directions.

From a nearby hillside, Texie searched the outlaw camp for the leader. Over the years, she'd memorized Snarly Pete's wanted poster and studied the witness accounts from his various devilish acts. He was a wiry little fellow, with skinny chicken legs and a bum arm that he kept close to his side in such a way that few even realized that it didn't work like it should. Weakness of any kind was a liability for a criminal leader.

A likely suspect emerged from behind a huge oak tree, making a run for the low earthen lodge. A taller, younger man dashed alongside him. He looked like he was assisting the suspect. That young man . . . he had light brown hair and a fine Texan cowboy hat—

What the hell? Was that . . . *Alec?*

Relief sank her belly and made her head swim. Randy hadn't left him dead in a ditch, thank God. He was all right—perfectly safe, in fact. As long as one didn't count the bullets zinging in his direction.

Which seemed a bit strange. Not that he would be in the thick of things, since he was *always* there. But that Randy seemed absent and it didn't look like Alec had been taken captive, either. No, he looked like a willing participant in helping Snarly Pete. A white-hot cannon ball of rage replaced relief. He was playing fast and loose like he always did. The bastard.

She pointed her pistol at him, sighted his big, fat head, and followed the bead.

Why, all she had to do was squeeze the trigger. Life would be so much simpler then. No more squirrelly stomach or fluttering throat. No more red-tinged irritation or deep-down outrage.

No more trouble. No more . . . Alec.

The thought of that made her fluttering throat close up.

A moment later, he and Snarly Pete disappeared underneath the porch of the earthen lodge that sat at the edge of the camp.

A couple of shotguns blew buckshot by her face. She glimpsed double barrels poking out from behind adjoining scraggly young oaks.

"I'm hit!" Roger squealed.

He clutched at his shoulder, his face twisted in agony. Texie sprang to his side and batted his hands away.

"Lemme see."

She peeled aside the shredded flannel print to find that a handful of pellets had peppered the meat of his right shoulder. She swallowed the squirt of saliva that preceded a retching bout. Not now, dammit! A few smears of blood, that's all it was. With any luck, that was all she'd see on her side.

"It ain't even bleedin'. Don't worry none about it. Get back out there."

Roger gave her a baleful look, so she shoved him back toward the fray. He limped ahead, his abused foot still big enough that they had to slice open the side of his boot to accommodate it.

Milo motioned to the left and held up three fingers. She

nodded and indicated to the right.

"Follow me, boys!" She pushed through the brush ahead of them.

She leapt down the last ten feet of the hillside and ran right through a bush that she hoped was not poison oak. Fifty yards off and they'd be in the middle of the outlaw camp. Fifty beyond that and they'd be on the front porch of that earthen lodge.

"Down!" she urged.

Her men streamed past her, spread out like fingers on a hand. She charged straight at a greasy-looking dude and stuck her revolver up his nose.

"Drop your gun!"

He flung his pistol aside like it was on fire. She yanked his hands behind his back lest he reconsider. Fastest gun in the West. That was the crap they spewed in dime novels. She'd practiced in the mirror, all right, but with something much more useful. Handcuffs. She whipped them out, snapped them around his thick wrists, and jammed her foot into the back of one knee. His knees buckled.

"Don't move or I'll shoot you!"

"Y–y–yes, ma'am."

He must never have seen the likes of her.

Few had.

She'd no more than finished congratulating herself than a howling madman barreled out of a nearby lean-to and rushed her. His fingers were stretched out like claws. She had just enough time to leap out of the way and grab Miss Jennie's barrel. This gave her a good grip by which to smack him on the back of his wild cloud of kinked hair. His howls changed from rage to pain.

Roger and Milo descended on him. Texie flipped her gun right side up in time to snap off a couple of shots at the two grubby villains hiding behind adjacent young oaks. They countered by firing back. One of their bullets took off a thimbleful of hair next to her ear. Another clanged off Miss Jennie's barrel, making it jitter and ring so violently that she lost feeling in her hand.

No problem, that. She took the gun in her left hand and triggered a couple of shots that went whirring off into the atmosphere.

A stray bullet hit the dust at her feet. She dashed for the big tree at the center of camp. Pandemonium everywhere. Outlaws cursed and yelled as posse members pounced at them. A red-haired maniac took to ringing the dinner bell like he was calling Satan and his four henchmen to dinner. In his other hand, he fired a pistol willy-nilly.

As she ran, she fumbled in her bandolier for replacement bullets. By the time she hit her destination, the relative safety of the bole of the gigantic tree, she had the chamber flipped open. Two, four, six. She slid the bullets into the chamber, then flipped the barrel shut. Her fingers shook like they always did when she was in a tizzy, so she forced herself to breathe and commanded them to stop that foolishness. They did so in short order. Just as she raised the business end of the gun toward the bell-ringing maniac, a rough hand closed around her upper arm.

Her chest seized up. A tall man all in black. Stovetop hat. Grizzled beard and eyebrows that twisted and flared out like porcupine quills.

"Stovetop Joe!" she blurted out.

"John Henry Frankfurter, actually. Do not shoot, sister. That will allow the devil traction in your soul. Violence only begets violence!"

"But you shot at me and Alec not a week ago!"

He grimaced, shoulders sagging. "I let rage cloud my vision." The posture vanished as he stood straight again, eyes filled with holy fire. "I have seen the error of my ways, sister. Those who live by the sword will die by it. My flock must learn that, too!"

With that, he stepped out from behind his hiding place, right out in the center of the madness.

"Stovetop! You'll be killed!"

A sweaty face appeared beside her. She jerked back, scared half to death. A young man with perfect white teeth grinned at her. She recognized him with a start—another of the Methodists. The least objectionable looking of the Murder Twins.

"John Henry's done filled with the Spirit, missus Sheriff. Jesus and the archangels will protect him! He's a powerful force for good."

She cringed as Stovetop Joe/John Henry stood at his full height. He stretched out one long arm that gripped a Bible like a pennant.

"Cease this violence!" he roared. "These men are the Lord's children! I call on you, men of the law, to yield to a higher power—"

One of said Lord's children leapt at John Henry and hooked an arm around his throat, using him as a shield. He hadn't dragged him five feet before John Henry twisted out of the outlaw's grasp and wailed on his head with his big black Bible. He kept on even when the outlaw fell to the ground, hands shielding his head. The Murder Twins rushed over to kick him in the ribs.

Rancho and his men made it off the hill to appear at the far end of the camp, guns blazing. They surprised a couple of outlaws who had been heading for the horses. In short order, those two ate lead for an eternal dinner and fell over in a heap.

A fistfight erupted. Careful examination of the dust cloud that rose up around the mass of men showed that three of Texie's posse were gaining the upper hand. Good, then. Now it was time to cut off the head of this beast—Snarly Pete. Whom Alec accompanied.

She made a run for the north side of the earthen lodge. The side that didn't have three guns thrust out of the windows, firing at various and sundry folks. The shooters didn't seem too discriminating when it came to whom they hit. At least one of the outlaws gave an agonized howl as a bullet buried itself in his right butt cheek.

Texie expected to feel the slap and burn of a bullet strike with every step, but she kept her eyes fixed on her goal. Finally, she lunged toward the wall and flattened her back against it. Her breath heaved. Before she had a chance to think too much about it, she crept to the back corner and peeked around it. Sure enough, a door sat along that wall, right next to a garbage pile that swarmed with flies.

The latch was a quiet affair, thank heavens. She opened the door wide enough to slip into a kitchen stacked high with flour sacks and cookpots. A pan of chocolate cake sat cooling on the top of a beat-up old stove. It sure smelled good. She'd been too nervous to eat last night or this morning. The rest of the place was not so fragrant, damp, dark, and musty.

The God-awful loud report of shotguns, rifles, and pistols blasted from the main room. She concealed herself in the doorway and risked a glance. The interior was dark and close, the weight of the earth all around making it seem like a cave. Illumination came from the windows where three men stood, their backs to her. One of them was Snarly Pete, and each of them sniped rounds from a firearm at the chaos outdoors.

"Damn it!" Snarly Pete exclaimed. "Hit another of ours! Good thing there's plenty of 'em."

By now, her eyes had adjusted to the dim light. The man at the window furthest to the left looked at Snarly Pete like he was insane. She'd recognize that sharp jawline anywhere.

Alec.

He noticed her in the doorway immediately, and his eyes got as big as a Brahman's balls. With frantic motions, he directed her to get back, out of the house.

She countered with a protruding middle finger. He looked so shocked that she nearly laughed. She glanced around the tiny kitchen. A walking stick propped against the door frame caught her eye. She grabbed it up and pantomimed bashing it over the heads of both Snarly Pete and the other shooter.

Alec shook his head with a wordless *No!*

He jabbed his finger from her to Snarly Pete and the other shooter, then held out a hand and made the figure of a running person with his index and middle fingers. Apparently, he wanted her to run off, away from trouble.

She held her sides and simulated laughing her head off, then pointed at him and mimicked the running figure with her fingers. *He's* the one who should run away. He shook his head violently, then straightened abruptly and froze. Snarly Pete had interrupted his murderous rampage to look Alec in the face. Alec looked about ready to expire from a heart attack.

"You having some sort of seizure, young feller?"

"Err . . . it comes and goes, Mr. Pete. Just a bit of the apoplexy." He inched toward the kitchen and Texie. "Just need a little air and I'll be fine."

"Do what you want. Yer a right terrible shot, anyhow." With a cackle, Snarly Pete returned to blasting away with his six iron.

Alec leapt for the kitchen and seized Texie's arm. Before she could twist away, he bundled her out the back door, shielding her from the others' view as he did so.

As soon as they closed the back door, she shoved him hard enough that he fell against it with a *thump.* "Get your hands offa me! To think I trusted you! Then I turn around and you're protecting that evil fiend!"

"Now hold on there, wildcat. I am not protecting him. I'm trying to keep you from getting shot!"

"What about my posse? You don't seem to care about shooting them up!"

He drew back, affronted. "I shot the dirt and the stack of firewood and the tail feathers of a chicken or two, but I did not shoot your men! How could you think I would—"

A wild shot whistled into the mud and stick roof directly above them, sending a shower of debris down on both of their heads. Alec seized her collar and pulled her into his chest to shelter her from the danger.

She growled and pushed him away, still angry as a polecat poked with a stick.

Exasperation tinged his voice. "Texie, please. You need to get back to your side. I'll take care of Snarly Pete. He won't suspect me."

She narrowed her eyes. "And why is that? Because you're in cahoots with him?"

"No, because he's my ticket to finding Randy again."

Randy. God, how she hated that murdering swine. Not enough to allow catching him to interfere with apprehending Snarly Pete, though.

She grasped the door latch. "Get out of my way."

He didn't move. "Texie, you don't understand. I can't let you blow his head off."

She tugged at his arm, but it felt like cast iron. She ground her bootheel into the earth to gain traction and tried again.

"Texie, stop it, would you? You're going to get both of us killed—"

At that moment, an outlaw ran around the side of the lodge.

Alec stabbed a finger at the newcomer. "See?"

The man, a squirrelly fellow covered in dried mud, gaped at them. He held a bow and arrow. To Alec, he said, "Hey, she's with them lawmen!"

He raised the bow and drew back the arrow to point it at Texie's head.

Alec cursed. He flung himself at the outlaw. The two of them collided and fell over, struggling.

Huh. Now that was an awfully sweet, chivalrous—albeit dumb—thing for him to do. While he was distracted, she slipped in the back door. Gun at the ready, she took up her post next to the interior door jamb again and peered into the main room.

The front door stood wide open. Through it, she saw Snarly Pete and his minion hurrying into the yard. The two of them cocked their revolvers and fired round after round in a cloud of smoke.

Texie snuck out the front door and up behind Snarly Pete. He continued blasting at the posse, unawares, until she jammed her pistol into the back of his neck.

"What the—"

"Drop your gun, you withered old pimple! You're under arrest."

He craned his neck over his shoulder to get a look at her. "I ain't givin' up to some little female. Horace! Help me out here!" He called to his companion, who couldn't hear on account of the fact that he was still shooting.

A lot of things happened at once.

Snarly Pete whipped around and swiped at her with the back of his stick-like arm. Horace realized what was happening and lunged toward them, eyes wide and mouth open in a soundless O. Snarly Pete bashed Texie in the ribs solidly enough that she staggered back. Her right arm swung wide and her trigger finger twitched. A round exploded out of the chamber and impacted a rotten oak branch in the canopy above them.

One bullet was all it took. A tremendous *snap* sounded from above. Texie glanced up in time to see a tree branch as it hurtled down toward them. She didn't even have a chance to scream before it landed atop all three of them with a loud *thwomp*.

Texie's head rang. Her eyes were open, but everything went black.

So. She was headed toward Perdition like she'd always suspected.

Chapter 24

Everything happened with exaggerated slowness, like a broken slide machine in those naughty camera booths in the backs of saloons and other dissolute places. Except that instead of half-clothed vixens with come-hither looks on their faces, Alec saw Texie struggling for her life against Snarly Pete. A gun or two blasted, then half a tree crashed down atop them with a great crack. A loud *swoosh* sounded as the branches impacted the ground, and a cloud of dust kicked up.

Alec's heart seized and dropped into his stomach. Somehow, it still managed to propel his body as he leapt toward Texie. His bootheels cracked twigs and smashed acorns. Tough, pointed oak leaves shredded his sleeves and hands as he dug into the fallen mess, frantic.

"Texie!" someone yelled, panicked.

Oh, that was him.

A glimpse of dark hair under a fist-thick, heavily-leafed branch. Hope surged in his chest like a wild, uncontrollable thing. Dread followed in a cold wind. What if . . . ?

A slight stirring and a muffled voice. "Here . . . "

Alec swiped at the limb, breaking off smaller branches in a frenzy until he uncovered her. Leaves and dirt were tangled in her silken hair. He got ahold of the limb at the junction of a good-sized branch and pulled with all his might. It lifted in an unwieldy, God-awful heavy clump. With a tremendous cry, he pushed it aside, off her. She lay, stunned and flattened on the ground. He plucked her up and gathered her in his arms, trying not to clutch her too firmly.

"Sweetheart, don't you be hurt, you hear me? Don't be hurt!"

She coughed. "I'm fine."

He let out a relieved breath. Another explosion of gunfire zeroed in on the earth at their feet and pinged into the downed limb.

Alec made a sound like "*Glurp!*" and swept Texie off her feet. He sprang behind the tree trunk where they found a moment's safety.

He looked down at her, encircled softly and warmly—and covered in tree sap—in his arms. She tipped her chin up, displaying a goose egg on her forehead and a scrape along her cheekbone. Her eyes, though . . . they snared him with invisible hooks and sucked him into a relentless vortex of deep, velvet brown, mystery upon mystery. He suspected that he'd never pull himself free from her.

"Texie?" His voice sounded like a hoarse, desperate carica-ture.

Her cheeks flamed. She gave a hitching breath then notice-ably composed herself.

"I'm . . . you can put me down."

He set her down on the ground gently then buried his sweaty face in her neck, unable to stop himself. She leaned against the tree trunk, but when she tried to stand on her own, her knees gave way. He propped her up.

"I've got you."

She touched the back of his neck and splayed her fingers into his hair. The motion sent shivers down his spine.

Snarly Pete's muffled voice exclaimed from somewhere underneath the mass of branches, "God-blasted hell, Horace. Get me out of here, you lousy excuse for a butler!"

Horace mumbled something incomprehensible that proved he remained among the living.

Steady on her feet now, Texie extracted herself from Alec's arms.

Alec took a good look at the camp. The screams, yells, and gunfire were diminishing as at least a half-dozen men lay scattered about. Some moaned and cursed while others lay still. Milo and Roger dragged three outlaws over to a tight knot of men who stood in a circle, hand in hand. One of the hand-holders let go. Rancho, distinctive with a red- and white-checkered bandanna around his neck, hollered and indicated his rifle butt.

"Grab it again, mister, or I'll wallop you good!"

The outlaw's eyes got as big and round as the face of a blooming sunflower and he grabbed his companion's hand again. Rancho looped a rope around their wrists and behind their backs, making mean knots as he did so. He must have been a cowhand at some time in the past to have such skill.

Snarly Pete's surly, muffled voice came from underneath the branches. "Horace! I'm waiting, and you know I don't like to wait when there's folks to be killed!"

Alec and Texie kicked the branches aside enough to uncover Snarly Pete's skinny, pinioned self.

"Get that tin star away from me!" Snarly Pete pointed at Texie and the shiny, though askew, star on her breast.

Before he could scoot away, the two of them hauled him to

standing.

"Squirrels are getting me!" Horace screeched from under a nearby branch. "Help!"

Texie nodded at Alec. "Get him. I've got this wriggly weasel."

Snarly Pete's mouth fell open to display broken, tobacco-stained teeth. "I ain't no—"

Horace flailed around to disturb the branches atop him. Alec hauled him to his feet and turned around.

His stomach flipped.

Snarly Pete held a foot-long Bowie knife to Texie's left breast. Over her heart. She stood as still as a deer scenting a predator.

"Hee-hee!" Snarly Pete laughed with glee. "I got her good, young feller!"

Alec forced his face still. "Now don't get hasty there, Mr. Pete. Why, look at her. That's a damn fine jug you're poking at. It would be a crime to ruin it."

Snarly Pete grunted. "Rather have me my freedom than a fine piece like this here missy. Come on, son. Pick Horace up and let's skedaddle. You help me get out of here and I'll tell you anythin' you want about Randy P."

Alec's tongue stuck to the roof of his mouth. He thought of all the work he'd gone through to get here, to Snarly Pete. He recalled the scheming and reversals, and now, finally, *finally,* here was the payoff he'd worked toward. The old lecher had turned out to be just as much the key to Randy's whereabouts as Alec had hoped. But that didn't take Texie into account. And if there's one thing he'd learned since he met that she-cat, it was that he'd better take her into account.

Alec nodded and took Texie's arm.

But as soon as Snarly Pete removed the Bowie knife from her breast, Alec pulled her back and behind him, sheltering her with his body.

"You snake!" Snarly Pete yipped.

At that moment, Rancho yelled, "Eeeeee yaw!"

He swung a looped coil of rope in a wide circle over his head, then flung it. Horace yelled as the lasso fell in a perfect circle around his middle. Rancho yanked it tight and dragged Horace straight into a ten-feet-tall stand of sticker bushes. He howled like an ugly, angry baby. Alec could practically see his half-decayed teeth from his angle.

"Durn it, Horace. You can't even escape right!" Snarly Pete hollered.

He plucked his Bowie knife out of its sheath and threw himself at Alec and Texie. Alec defended himself by grabbing Snarly Pete by his scrawny but surprisingly strong wrists. They whirled around, struggling.

Texie grabbed Snarly Pete by the back of his shirt like a bronco buster holds onto his saddle. The three of them lurched this way and that until Texie managed to pounce on Snarly Pete's back. The motion knocked Alec flat on his buttocks.

Snarly Pete clawed at Texie with his one good arm like a bear trying to brush off a hive of stinging honey bees. She clung to his back and struggled to wind an arm around his neck. When she managed to put the crook of her elbow at his windpipe, she levered her other arm and tightened her grip. He gurgled.

Alec thrust out his leg. Snarly Pete tripped over it and went down in a painful-looking splat.

Texie rode his back on the way down, smacking her knees on the hard earth. But true to form, she didn't let a bit of pain faze her. A smile of pure little-girl glee split her face.

"Got him! Rancho! Alec! He's ours!"

Alec couldn't help but laugh. An instant later, Rancho and

Milo appeared and converged on Snarly Pete. Between Texie and them, they wrestled the old codger to his feet. He wheezed for a minute before he got his breath back. When he did, he was spitting mad. Since his arms were restrained behind his back, he thrust his wattled chin at Alec. His bitty little eyes shone black like the portal to hell.

"You'll never find Randy P now! I'd sooner roast in hell than turn him over to a traitor like you!"

It took all four of them to lasso Snarly Pete so that his struggling, cursing form was contained. Milo took hold of Horace, and Rancho guided Snarly Pete by the arm to march both of them toward the group of other prisoners.

She stretched her shoulders back and groaned, massaging a sensitive spot on her neck. Alec laid his palm atop her shoulder and rubbed the place for her. After all the shooting and running around and that damn branch falling on her, he just wanted to put his hands on her to make sure she was solid and alive and not too angry at him. He had no more than thought that before she rewarded him with a sigh of pleasure.

Alec took her by the elbow, and they headed toward the knot of prisoners and posse members just in time to see Rancho cram a bandana in Snarly Pete's mouth and tie another one around his head to keep it in place. That effectively shut him up.

The posse greeted them with cheers and back-slaps.

"I never seen nothin' like that!" crowed Jack Daw. "It's downright inspiring." He wiped a tear away, smudging the considerable amount of dirt on his face as he did so.

John Henry, lean and sour-faced as ever, stood tall. "Let us thank the Lord for this blessing!"

Alec, Texie, and the posse shut up momentarily as everyone

looked at one another. Well, why not?

"Here's to God, Jesus, and the heavenly host!" Alec proclaimed. "Hooray!"

"Hooray!" the crowd responded.

Texie's eyes danced when she looked at him. He took that as an invitation to wrap his arms around her and swing her around and around until dizziness forced him to stop. When Alec's eyes righted, he saw Texie smiling up at him.

"You had me fooled for a bit, there. I shoulda known that you wouldn't up and turncoat without a plan to turn back."

He waggled his eyebrows at her. "Most certainly. I want Randy if I can get him." He lowered his lips to her ear and spoke only for her. "But there's someone else I want even more."

The smile left her face and she looked down at the ground. "Why do you have to say such things?"

"Why don't you believe them?"

Color rose in her cheeks. "This isn't the time or the place for fol-der-ol, Malone."

He couldn't think of a better time, but he let it be for now.

Alec spent the next hour helping to round up the last of the gang. A dozen of the outlaws suffered from gunshot wounds with varying degrees of severity. Rancho was appointed the resident doctor due to his favorite remedy—whiskey. He dumped it on wounds and down gullets, and it seemed to cure whatever could be cured. Four of the outlaws had been killed outright. A couple of others looked like they might not survive the night, but the forty-odd who remained were more or less alive.

On their side, Fred Harkins lay on the ground, unconscious after someone took the paddle of a butter churner to his head.

A few others had flesh wounds, and one of Rancho's men had a broken arm. That was it for casualties. For the amount of gunplay and general misbehavior that had gone on, the damage seemed light.

Alec kept an eye on the Methodists, not trusting them to refrain from taking vengeance on him, but they seemed more occupied with tending to the wounded and hauling up fresh buckets of cool spring water from the well. He stuck close to Texie, too. He couldn't help but feel like the moon to her earth, caught in her orbit, endlessly circling. Once, he would have minded another person having so much power over him. Now, he didn't.

Texie rested against a barrel filled with salt pork and pulled on her freshly refilled canteen. He took the canteen from her when she was finished. Shooting, running around, and arresting folks were sweaty work.

John Henry sat on a crate nearby. He took his stovepipe hat off and wiped at the sweat beading his forehead.

"It's good of you to help out, Mr. Henry," Texie said. "Alec and I thought for sure that the gang had skinned you alive. But here you are, preaching to the unworthy and assisting the unwise. I have to hand it to you. I am impressed."

He considered her, then squinted at Alec. Alec tried not to squirm under his penetrating gaze.

Texie continued on. "That said, I'm still charging you with attempted murder for shooting at Alec when you first came upon us."

John Henry's stoic expression did not change. His eyes were onyx under the black and white fringe of gnarled eyebrows. After a moment, he nodded.

"You are well within your rights to do so, Sheriff. Bilbo Joe,

Wilbur Joe, and I will make amends for our misdeeds as the law allows."

Alec put a hand over his mouth to stop the guffaw that nearly burst out. He had plenty of grievances with his parents, but at least they had not given him a name like Bilbo Joe.

"I appreciate the cooperation. I surely do. Enough that I will overlook the 'aiding and abetting fugitives of the law' charge if you'll see fit to testify against these men at their trials."

"Hey!" Alec protested.

Texie and John Henry ignored him.

"That seems fair, Sheriff. I'll see to it that Wilbur Joe and Bilbo Joe do as you ask also. I suppose we can even forgive the grievance we have against that scoundrel." He nodded at Alec.

"Well, aren't you generous?" Alec sniped. "I've got a grievance myself, Mister. You and your minions from hell don't deserve to be out and about, attacking innocent people—"

"Alec," Texie said.

"All right. *Mostly* innocent people—"

"Alec!"

"What?"

She looked irritated. He raised his hands in self-defense.

"Fine. I guess I can forgive his attempt at murder for you, sweetheart." He narrowed his eyes at John Henry. "This time."

John Henry bowed his head with something like grace and strode off to get back to work.

Texie nudged his arm. She grinned. "Thank you."

He raised his eyebrows at her. She shrugged. "Guess you're rubbing off on me."

He dropped his voice. "Oh, I'll rub something—"

"Shut up, Alec."

He was just about ready to persuade her to make better use of her sweet mouth when a shout went up. Roger jabbed a finger across the canyon to the crowded brush.

"I saw someone! Left of the bald-faced rocks!"

The whole posse scoured the hillside with their eyes.

"There!" Milo called.

Alec followed his line of sight. About a quarter-mile up the hillside, he saw a white face jerk to the side as if in response to Milo's words. Who . . . ? When he recognized the man's movement, he straightened like a schoolmarm hearing her pupils cuss.

"It's Randy!"

"Get him!" Rancho bellowed to the posse members. His words prompted a flurry of activity.

By the time Alec jammed his hat back on his head and grabbed his canteen by the strap, a half-dozen men from the posse had run on ahead, brandishing weapons.

Alec took two steps after them, then stopped. Texie hadn't moved from where she'd been standing at the start of the commotion. The smile had left her face.

"What are you waiting for? Go after him."

Alec wanted to do just that. He knew he *should* go after Randy. Catch that rotten apple around his worm-infested belly and force him to cough up what he owed Alec. But there was a problem with that scenario. Alec's legs would not move.

Texie crossed her arms over her belly. "Ain't he the whole reason you're here? Don't give up now. Go get the bastard."

He forced himself to relax into a casual pose, even though sweat sprang up on his neck.

"Nah. I like the view here better." His voice cracked despite his best efforts.

Their eyes met. Emotion surged like a symphony, aching and beautiful.

Her chin began to tremble. She flicked her eyes away and her voice quieted.

"You need to go, Alec. I know it's what you want, what brought you all the way out to Abalone in the first place, much less out here after these miscreants."

He drew closer to her. She flinched but stood her ground. "You're right. He was what I wanted when I came out here."

He put two gentle fingers under her chin and nudged her gaze to his. "Found something better, though."

"Oh, come on, Alec. The two of us go together as well as porcupines and petticoats. We don't have a future. Heck, we barely have a present—"

Lord knows what else she had to say. He pressed his lips to hers and all that talk turned to a "Mmpfh?"

The future. Yessiree. It held a lot of questions. But for right now, the only answers he needed were right here in the warm, sweet press of their lips.

Chapter 25

T he Children of Israel wandered in the desert for forty years before they reached civilization. It wasn't quite that bad for Texie as she led the ragtag group of outlaws and posse members into Abalone after three days' time. The amount of complaining, moaning, and outright weeping that occurred along the way made her *feel* like it had been forty years, though.

As they approached Main Street, Alec caught her eye and gave her a warm smile that made her insides go weak. She tried not to think too much about their future. Mainly because they didn't have one. He was a thief and a rogue, a troublemaker and a mischief-causer. And he wasn't likely to change any time soon. People didn't change. Oh, sure, they tried every now and again, but that didn't mean it worked.

Still, she couldn't help but want to burrow into his heart and curl up there for a nap like a contented cat.

Aww, what a load of foolishness.

The kids playing at the edge of town saw them coming and alerted the rest of the town, who lined the street to welcome them home with cheers, smiles, and raised glasses of beer. Even Carlene and her stable full of fallen women waved at them with glee. Carlene looked as impeccable and gorgeous as always. Today, she wore a fine violet confection with bone-colored lace at her neck and the bottom of her skirt. The rich purple shimmered in the sun. And here Texie was, dirty and grungy, with a scraped cheek, bumped head, and sticks tangled in her hair. She could pretty much guarantee that she did not smell of French perfume like Carlene.

Alec didn't seem to notice Carlene on account of being too occupied with strutting like a royal peacock. He grinned and nodded in such a way that whipped the crowd into an even greater frenzy.

One fellow did notice Carlene. Wilbur Joe, that looker of a Methodist who walked alongside John Henry and Bilbo Joe. The three of them trailed behind everyone, severe in their all-black clothing and hats. John Henry didn't give the crowd a second glance, but Wilbur Joe gawped at Carlene like he'd been struck in the head by a fencepost.

Carlene lifted her chin and smiled at him. No doubt, he'd get a hefty discount if he visited her ladies this evening.

Beauregard Gleason didn't look too happy with the doings. He leaned against the hitching post in front of the half-burned Crystal Palace, thin, greasy black hair protruding from under his new bowler, a frown on his pockmarked chin. His frown deepened when he spied Alec.

Yes, the snow globes. He must have figured out what happened to them.

She'd have to do something about them, too. Sometime after she booked forty-odd outlaws into a jail fit to hold four—if they were on the thin side.

In the meantime, she snatched a mug of beer off some half-drunk cowboy and downed a healthy swig. The cowboy reached for an amorous embrace. Alec inserted himself between the two of them like a pup demanding a pet.

Texie offered Alec the rest of the beer mug. That earned her a laugh and a gentle guiding touch at the small of her back. She tried not to notice it too much lest she drag him off behind the saloon and put his lips to better use.

Texie, the town council, and four recently appointed deputies commandeered the Crystal Palace, much to Gleason's sweaty objections.

"What's the difference, Beauregard?" shrilled the stalwart postmistress general. "You can't get anybody up there to see your girls or drink your whiskey until them naughty pictures get fixed anyhow."

Because apparently, the smoke from the recent blaze smeared soot all over Gleason's prized portraits of half-clad ladies in such a way that the buxom lasses looked like bearded lumberjacks.

Gleason had tried to fix the problem with some elbow grease and old rags, but that only resulted in scraping the paint away, so now he had either headless women or bearded ones and business had declined sharply as a result.

Once he realized that his objections about the use of the Crystal Palace for a jail were getting him nowhere, he decided on taking a trip to El Paso to retrieve a talented painter or two to fix up his paintings and add various and sundry naked pictures around the place. Texie watched as he boarded the noon stage. He and Alec were having an intense conversation about some mysterious subject.

Much of the afternoon passed in a flurry of duties. The arrests meant reams of paperwork. She also had to send for the traveling judge, figure out how to feed everyone, and have deputies escort them to the outhouses in orderly rows.

Between all this, Texie barely had the chance to notice that Alec and his handsome face had made themselves scarce.

Eventually, things were mostly sorted, with guards at the doors and patrolling around the saloon in case someone climbed out the windows. Texie warned the outlaws that such an action would result in their privates being peppered with buckshot, a fate that seemed worse than death to most of them. Snarly Pete, Horace, and a couple of the other fellows occupied the proper jail cells. On account of their special status as pains in the ass.

As the shadows lengthened into night, Texie took a well-earned sit-down on the bench outside the mercantile exchange. Mama Carmen brought out dinner, a tortilla stuffed with beans and covered in mole sauce.

As with every time she had something to eat, Herman the Hound appeared out of nowhere. He trotted toward her, head bowed low as his scruffy tail swished from side to side.

"You lousy little mutt." She grinned at the sight of him despite herself.

He pushed his head into her hand. His efforts got some scratches and a hunk of the burrito. Her breakfast had consisted of coffee, and her lunch of licorice sticks and a handful of roasted goober peas, so the dinner tasted like heaven on earth. She was wiping her mouth off when that broken-down wretch, Ralph, came loping down Main Street toward her, Alec riding him bareback.

His face lit up when he caught sight of her, and she couldn't help but blush a bit. He dismounted Ralph a bit more skillfully than in the past, landing with a grunt and a *huff* in the dust. He set his valise next to the bench and propped his foot atop it, eyeing Herman.

"That's the ugliest dog I've ever seen."

Herman didn't care. He wagged his tail and wiggled around.

"You like ugly, don't you?" She nodded at Ralph.

"Point taken."

Chigger Antoine gave a holler as he fell off the boardwalk across the street, drunk and happy as he ever was. The ruckus caught Alec's attention. As he looked, the late afternoon sun illuminated the blond in his eyelashes and the smooth masculine curve of his jaw.

A terrible pang stabbed her in the heart. She wanted him like a wildfire wants to burn dry weeds. But he could destroy her in the same way, quick and thoughtless and on his way to some other town or city, some other scheme, leaving a trail of broken-hearted idiots like herself.

She examined the uneven boards beneath her feet and struggled to keep calm as the blood heated her face. The longing was worse than before, ever since she'd felt his arms around her, his scent an aphrodisiac.

When she glanced up, his eyes were on her face, his lips—those devilish lips—crooked up in a grin.

"I've got something to show you."

He slid onto the bench beside her and propped his valise on his knees. With a flick of the catch, he opened the bag and pushed aside the shirt and ties. A pair of specially made European snow globes shone in all their glassy glory.

"You . . . what? You're giving them up, just like that?"

"Well, why wouldn't I?" His voice rose with indignation. "I'm doing it for you, darlin'. And you're worth it. I aim to show you that—and keep showing you."

He sounded so earnest. So persuasive. He moved closer to her, and his voice fell an octave. "You're inspiring all these strange feelings in me, peach blossom. Lawfulness. Sacrifice. Love—"

She jumped to her feet. "Don't say that!" She yelped like scalded dog and jerked back out of arms' reach.

His eyes clouded in confusion. "I thought you wanted them back?"

"Of course I want them back!"

"Then why are you shouting?" He was on his feet now, too. His ice blue eyes looked colder than a glacier. "I have been thinking, Texie. Hard. About you and what you want outta me. I'm trying to be a better man. To show you that I'm willing to do what you want."

"It's not just what I want. It's what's right. But now I have to throw you back in jail. You already belong there for escaping from jail in the first place."

"Nah. You don't need to worry about that. Me and Mr. Beauregard Gleason had a little conversation before he left town. I explained how I was just keeping the globes safe from the conflagration since I knew how much he loved them. He promised to drop the charges no questions asked if they appeared back in the display case when he returns. Which they will as soon as all those grubby outlaws get themselves hauled off to the state prison."

"How did you . . . ? Never mind. I have a feeling I don't really want to know."

"No, you don't, Texie. That's pretty clear, it seems. I'm willing to give up the snow globes for you. My freedom. My life. Doesn't that make you happy?"

"No, it doesn't make me happy! Why would I want some man who finds it a chore to be with me?"

"That's not what I meant—"

"Maybe not. But that's the way it is." She bit down on her lip to keep from spewing out more crazy, angry, frightened words.

He sighed and held his hands up in surrender, then stepped in way too close. "Texie."

If she let it, the low, sweet sound of his voice would crack away the last shards of ice which encased her heart. And then where would she be? Up Shit Creek, that's where.

"I can't right now, Alec. I'm tired. My head hurts and my throat is raw from all the orders I've been giving, and I just want to go to sleep in my bed for once instead of on top of a prickly pear. We can part company tomorrow, after I get myself together a bit more."

"Part company!"

"Tomorrow, Alec. I'm set on that."

He threw his hands into the air in exasperation. "Damn me from here to Minneapolis. How much more you want out of me before you open up and let me in?" His voice sounded raw.

A woman's giggle floated down the street and broke the tension between them. Two people stood just clear of the light from the Desert Rose's windows. The low murmur of their voices revealed their identities. Carlene and Wilbur Joe.

Alec echoed her thoughts. "Is that the Methodist boy?"

It was the distraction she needed. She slipped away, hurrying toward her house before Alec could say anything more about it.

She braced herself for his hand catching her by the elbow to stop her, but it did not come. There was just an exhalation of breath and a defeated, pained sounding word. "Texie."

Herman the hound trotted alongside, faithful as always.

Before dawn, Texie rose from bed and stoked the stove. It

took a good thirty minutes of clattering around with the coffee pot and the kerosene lamp until her coffee was ready for the pat of butter she so enjoyed in it.

Like she had so many times in years past, she stood out on the back porch, leaning against a wooden support post, and watched the sun creep over the horizon with long purple fingers. She and Papa had watched sunrises together innumerable times over the years on this very porch. She could see him in her mind's eye even now, his grizzled, lined face browned from the sun, razor stubble along his strong chin, gingham shirt tucked in his worn-smooth Levi's.

They never needed to talk much at such times, though if she had something on her mind, he would always listen like the world revolved around her. She imagined that for him, it did. He always made her feel that way, anyhow. Just like someone else she knew . . . except that Alec scared her, too.

If only she could talk out the tangled knot of thoughts and feelings wrapped around her brain and vital organs.

She looked around at the quiet desert that was her back yard, the darkened windows of the shops and homes around her. Even Herman had gone off somewhere, maybe hunting for jackrabbits or horny toads.

Well, then, she was most definitely alone.

"Papa, I've got something to say. Listen up from on high, will you? There's this rascal of a man I can't get out of my head . . ."

She went on telling him everything. It took a while and she rambled. She knew what he'd say, then, straight shooter that he was.

What are you asking me, girl?

"I'm asking what to do."

His dark eyes would bore into hers.

You do what's right.

"But I don't know what that is!"

He'd give her that little smile, with its crinkles at the corners of his eyes.

Oh, yes you do, pearl. I know that you do. It's usually the hard thing.

She considered that for a piece.

Ah, hell.

She went inside to wash her face and dab on a drop of Mama's nearly evaporated perfume. Then she brushed out her long hair until it shone and put her Sunday skirt on.

Alec's eyes widened when he saw her and traveled from her scrubbed cheeks all the way to her laced-up shoes. He was in front of her in a flash. She found him, unsurprisingly, in the Desert Rose, jawing with Jimmy the bartender, fancy boot resting on the foot rail.

"Good morning and hallelujah. I'm mighty happy to see you looking like such a vision of earthly perfection."

She cocked an eyebrow at him. "You're looking fit as a fiddle yourself."

He straightened his spine and flipped up his collar, spreading his plumage like a cock on the walk. "I'm happy to hear you at last acknowledge the fine figure of a man that I am."

Restraining herself from sighing and rolling her eyes took a concerted act of will. He must have noticed because he gave a little laugh. Then he took her hand.

"Come on, darlin'."

He led her out to the middle of the street and turned her around so they looked at the stagecoach to the left and the front of the Desert Rose just across from them. He nodded toward the stagecoach. The driver hefted up a heavy trunk, his face purple with effort.

Her face felt frozen, but she heard herself speak. "Randy's out there somewhere. I reckon you want to take off after him."

"Nah. I'm not very good at revenging myself. Not that I've forgiven him, mind you. But I got something to do here instead."

"I see. Prospecting for gold, isn't that it?" She probably should tell him that the only metal he was likely to find around here was the iron on the railroad tracks.

"Not like you're thinking. See that stagecoach?"

He was going to say that he was taking it. She knew it.

A ruckus started up down the street. Shouting and boot heels meeting the boardwalk. A blonde head peered out the stagecoach's window. Carlene? Wilbur Joe came stampeding toward it like an angry bull chased him.

It did.

John Henry hobbled like a stiff-legged demon, cane in one hand and the other one helping along his bum leg. There wasn't anything wrong with his lungs. "By God, boy, you are not running off with that harlot if I have anything to say about it!"

"You don't, Pa!" Wilbur Joe shouted back.

"Hurry, Angel!" Carlene flung the stagecoach door open.

Wilbur Joe leapt into the coach. John Henry kept coming. Only now, he was waving his cane around like a baseball bat.

"Go, you idiot!" Carlene bellowed to the driver. "Go!"

The driver scrambled for the four horse reins and yelled, "Giddyap!" Only the likes of an angry woman could have inspired the terror in his voice.

The coach took off before John Henry could catch it, clouds

of dust behind its creaking wheels. He gave a roar and took to banging his cane on the nearest horse trough in frustration.

"What in God's name is going on?" Texie asked.

"Carlene and Wilbur Joe are eloping."

She gaped at Alec.

"But what about the Desert Rose? She can't just leave it. Can she?"

Alec's grin could have dazzled a nun. "I am the new proprietor of that rather questionable but undeniably profitable establishment. You see, we worked out a deal this morning. She'll get fifty percent—"

Texie threw her arms around his neck and smashed her lips against his. They kissed for a long moment until the need for breath caused them to part, gasping into one another's mouth.

"So, you're staying?" For some reason, she needed to hear him say those words.

He smiled. "I am, sweetheart. I want you something fierce. More, even, than I want to play poker. And that's unprecedented, in my experience."

She grinned back. "Mine, too. I mean, I want you, too. You're the only man I've ever wanted like this."

They smiled at each other and kissed again. After a moment, she drew back enough to put a forearm's distance between them.

"Come with me," she said.

His eyes drew together in puzzlement. She reached around to give his fine, firm buttocks a pinch. Then, she winked.

"Do I need to tell you again?"

Before she had a chance to blink, they were at her front door. He opened it for her.

"Ladies first."

She liked the sound of that. Soon enough, she liked the feel of it, too.

Sad the story is over?

Giddyap over to join the author's mailing list and receive a **Free** Bonus Story in the Lady Law Universe! Subscribe at http://bit.ly/30qhIAS

About the Author

Xina Marie Uhl loves to make people laugh, study history, play with dogs, and eat pizza. Traveling the world is also high on her list of good things. Keep up on her writerly doings by joining her monthly newsletter for notifications about upcoming releases, special offers, and free fiction.

If you've made it this far and you enjoyed the book, why not review it? Short or long, your review helps to spread the word about the book.

You can connect with me on:
- http://www.xuwriter.com
- https://twitter.com/xuwriter
- https://www.facebook.com/XinaMarieUhl

Subscribe to my newsletter:
- http://bit.ly/30qhIAS

Also by Xina Marie Uhl

My work runs the gamut from romance and adventure to fantasy and humor. If you enjoyed this book, you'll probably get a kick from the ones listed below.

All Mouth and No Trousers
Behold dogsleds and penguins.

Howling winds and cold, pitiless wastes.

This is Antarctica, where the intrepid inhabitants of the frozen ends of the earth battle the terrain, and each other, to find love—in a past much like that of the early 1900s.

Whiter Pastures
The appearance • of handsome young Handy at the British Antarctic base sets reluctant spinster Florance all agog. But when she makes a disturbing discovery about him, she must decide whether she can summon the courage to carry out a daring, deadly, and hilarious plan.

Come, find love and lunacy in the frozen reaches of the earth!

The Cat's Guide to Human Behavior

At last, the mysteries of humans' strange habits and bizarre desires are revealed in this clever, timely guide for the modern cat.

Discover answers to timeless feline questions such as: Why does my human refuse to groom herself with her tongue? For decades felines have been meowing for such a guidebook—don't deny them any longer!

www.ingramcontent.com/pod-product-compliance
Lightning Source LLC
Chambersburg PA
CBHW030909060726
47591CB00005B/1467